Shadow Fae Magic

WICKED FAE
BOOK TWO

AMELIA SHAW

CHAPTER 1
AURELIA

Could I trust the man I'd left with? I wasn't sure and had no idea if would he tell me the truth anyway. *Probably not.*

Even so, there was no harm in asking.

I chewed my lip nervously and stared up at the huge man before me. "You won't tell Grey where I am?"

Asher peered at me incredulously, his eyes wide and eyebrows raised. "Of course, not. There's obviously a reason you're running from him."

I wasn't running, was I? And even if what Asher said was true, I had every right to run away from a bad situation. I'd been betrayed from the beginning. Grey only wanted me for a job, and he'd done whatever was necessary to bring me in, including all the lies he'd told me.

I was done with it all, him and his lies.

"I appreciate the offer, Asher. I really don't have anywhere else to go." That was the truth.

With that thought came a crushing loneliness. Was I making

a terrible mistake going with Asher? The riders were friends with Grey, not me. So why was Asher being so nice?

None of this made any sense. I eyed him warily. "Why are you helping me run from him?"

The elevator door dinged open, and Asher put out his arm to make sure it didn't close on us. Then he gestured for me to go out ahead of him. He didn't answer my question, and that fact wasn't lost on me.

The receiving room was empty. Everyone must still be down at the ring watching the horror show. Layla's gruesome death flashed in my mind, and I shuddered. She deserved what she'd gotten, of course, but that didn't make her demise any less disturbing.

My feet pattering on the tile floor was the only sound in the empty space as we raced through the receiving room and out the front doors. The sun beat down on us, blinding me after so long in the dark. But I took in deep breaths of the crisp air and sighed as happiness filtered through me.

I'd loved the forest from the moment I saw it for the first time. It felt like home.

Maybe I could just run into the forest and live out my days off the land. That wouldn't be too difficult, right? Who am I kidding?

I scanned the outside of the facility and groaned at what I saw there. Asher seriously wasn't expecting me to get on the back of that death machine, was he?

I blinked at the motorcycle as the hulking guy moved toward it, shaking my head as I stood there. There was no way in hell I was getting on that.

"If you want to get out of here, this is the only way, princess," Asher said as he strode towards the bike, throwing the words over his shoulder.

Well, shit.

I moved slowly, taking careful, tiny steps towards the motorcycle. My heart was pounding, and feelings of fear and anxiety were tinkling along my nerves.

Asher, the big brute, climbed on like it was the easiest thing in the world, and pushed up the kickstand as he waited for me to climb on.

It was this or face Grey again. My choice became no choice, really. "Fine, then," I huffed. I could die on a motorcycle, but at least death wouldn't break my heart again.

"Here." He grabbed a helmet and handed it to me.

I put the helmet on but fumbled with fastening it. Asher chuckled before turning and securing it under my chin with his thick, steady fingers. He tightened it with a final tug, being sure to test to make sure it was on properly.

"Thank you," I said, still wary of the huge machine. "How many motorcycles do you have? Don't you have a car?"

"No, I don't have a car," he said, rolling his eyes "And I have several bikes. Though one less, since we rescued you."

We both- knew I was stalling, but I needed to psych myself up to get on that thing. My hands were shaking, and my breathing was more like panting.

"Sorry about that," I said, glancing away. He'd lost his favorite bike to a fireball when they came to rescue me from Malcolm's house of horrors.

"It's fine, but we're running out of time if you want to get out of here before Grey comes after you." He raised an eyebrow at me and revved the engine for effect.

The bike rumbled ominously, the sound shivering along my spine, causing goose bumps to break out over my skin.

I blew out a shaky breath. It was now or never.

I moved to the bike and threw my leg over the huge machine then I grabbed onto the back of Asher's shirt, trying to keep a little distance between us. Having a different idea, he reached back and wrapped my arms around his waist.

"You need to hold on tight, especially if you're scared." He chuckled.

His ribcage was so wide my hands couldn't touch as I wrapped my arms around his waist. Instead, I gripped the front of his T-shirt as he started the engine.

He didn't warn me as he took off down the dirt road, he just did. A girly squeal escaped my mouth as I plastered my front to his back.

"A warning would have been nice!" I yelled over the roar of the engine.

Asher's deep laugh was his only response.

The trees flew by at high speed and the wind rushed by, whistling loudly.

The air beat at my face until I hid behind Asher's broad back, his body blocking most of the wind. I breathed deeply in an attempt to calm my racing nerves.

Asher's back suddenly tensed beneath my touch.

He was relaxed until now. What's wrong?

"Hold on, princess!" Asher's panicked shout made me tense and grip his shirt tighter.

"What's going on?" I peeked up over his shoulder to see a roadblock up ahead, but we weren't slowing down in the least.

Malcolm stood in the middle of the street on the other side of the ward. I flinched.

What the fuck? How did he find me?

An iridescent shield wove its way around Malcolm and blocked any kind of escape.

I glared at him when he smiled cruelly. He didn't care what happened to me anymore. It was obvious in the way he stood there, ready for me to crash into his shield.

The second we crossed the wards I screamed, "Stop!"

Asher skidded to a stop inches from Malcolm's shield, and the bike slid out from beneath us, kicking dust up in Malcolm's face.

I rolled across the dirt road, gravel digging into my skin, but I was otherwise unharmed as I jumped to my feet, magic lighting up my palms.

"Run, Princess!" Asher yelled.

"No," I growled back.

I can take care of myself. I'm not helpless.

I glared at Malcolm as the purple magic glowed in my hands. "Why are you here?" I yelled.

A smirk lit Malcolm's face. "You are mine and I have come to take you home... by force, if necessary."

"I would rather die than go anywhere with you." I threw magic at Malcolm's shield.

It hit the shield and bounced off, the magic crackling a few feet away from Malcolm but fizzling out without doing any damage.

Asher stood and put himself between me and Malcolm. "Run, Princess," he repeated.

"You sound like a broken record, Asher. I'm not running away." I shook my head and stepped to the side so I could see my enemy.

"Infuriating woman. I swear you'll be the death of me. You have one choice here, Aurelia. You run now, because in a few minutes Grey will be done with the assholes in the facility and he'll be on his way here," Asher said.

Shit. What will I do when I have to face Grey and Malcolm at the same time?

Malcolm stepped forward and held up his hand, which was crackling with energy. "You will not leave. I'm taking you home with me."

"I'm not going anywhere." I threw another ball of magic with the same result. "It would be a fair fight if you'd stop being a coward and drop the shield."

Malcolm laughed. "Why would I do that when I can get the same result from behind the safety of my shield?"

"There's no honor among the Fae," Asher growled.

Malcolm let his electric power crackle over his palm before he lobbed it in my direction.

Asher shoved me out of the way, and I rolled across the dirt road again.

"You can't get past his shield. You need to run, now!" Asher yelled.

He was right. Scanning the trees, I searched for a good place to get lost but not finding one. I scrambled up from the dusty ground and crouched low, moving quickly to the tree line. I had no intention of being caught by Malcolm again.

He'd treated me horribly when he kidnapped me before and he had plans for the future that I would rather die than endure. I would not allow him to capture me again.

The trees swayed in the breeze as if directing me the way I needed to go. It was strange but it felt like they were guiding me. I didn't stop to think about it, I just went. The sounds of fighting and shouting faded the longer I stumbled through the underbrush following the trees' direction.

What was I thinking? How could trees possibly be telling me where to go? It didn't make sense. "Where are you taking me?" I whispered.

I stopped to catch my breath and laid a hand on the nearest tree. The bark pulsed beneath my touch with urgency.

How do I know that it's trying to warn me?

The tree pulsed again, and the urgency increased. Someone was following me, and the tree didn't know if the presence was friend or foe. It urged me forward. I didn't have much choice but to do as it demanded.

What about Asher?

My steps faltered. Could he fight alone against the Fae

warrior? I wasn't sure. He wouldn't be able to get past Malcolm's shield either, so why did he stay behind?

It'll be for nothing if you don't move now.

I followed the trees deeper into the forest. The skin on the back of my neck prickled with unease. The tree was right. I was being stalked and I didn't know if it was by a threat.

The trees pulsed with more urgency. I stumbled in the direction they swayed and picked up my pace until I was running flat out.

I completely lost track of where I was going, running until my chest ached and I panted for breath.

I need to stop. I can't keep up this pace much longer.

My knees buckled and I crashed to the ground on my hands and knees, sucking in huge, heaving breaths. I really wasn't in great shape to be running like that.

A twig snapped in the distance. I flinched, scrambling up to my feet and calling magic to my palms.

"Easy, Princess," Asher said, stepping into view.

I blew out a shaky breath, relieved that it was only him. "Asher."

"Don't get too comfortable. Malcolm is still out there somewhere. The bastard got away." He clenched his hand into a fist at his side.

Asher's face was dirty and there was a cut above his brow that was trickling blood.

"Are you okay?" I took a tentative step forward.

"I'm fine, but we need to move." He turned back towards the direction he'd come from, expecting me to follow.

"Wait, the trees want me to go this way." I chewed my lip.

It sounded ridiculous even to my own ears. Asher raised a brow in question but thankfully didn't ridicule me or ask if I was crazy.

"Okay then, we follow the trees." He stepped forward and peered up at the trees swaying.

"Don't ask me how, I just know they want me to go this way." I shrugged.

"Some of the Fae have elemental magic that helps them communicate with the earth. It's rare and mostly among the royal bloodlines." He put a hand on my back to lead me in the right direction.

Oh, great. Just more proof that I was a royal Fae. Just what I needed.

"What happened back there?" I changed the subject, not wanting to talk about the elephant in the forest. I was still holding out hope that I wasn't who everyone said I was.

"Malcolm lost his shit when you ran and tried to go after you, but don't worry. I still have a few tricks up my sleeve." He winked at me with a broad grin.

I was never going to know all that the riders of the hunt could do. They were a secretive bunch. They wouldn't even tell me how they knew Grey.

My chest tightened at the thought of the shifter who'd betrayed me. He'd known from the beginning who the man was that caused all this, and he'd kept it from me. He lied to me about the role he played in my mother's death. How could I still miss him? How did I still want to be with him after that?

I stomped through the forest with Asher by my side in silence until a tingle ran down my spine.

"Do you feel that?" There was some kind of magic here that felt familiar.

"Magic," Asher breathed. "It's Fae magic."

What was Fae magic doing out in the middle of the forest? Had Malcolm found us?

Magic crackled in my palms as I continued through the trees.

A clearing came into view as I stepped beyond the trees. A

shimmering door of magic stood in the center of the field, and I frowned.

"What is that?" I whispered.

Asher's gaze snapped to mine before turning in the direction of the door. "What? I don't see anything but trees."

"There is a shimmering purple door right there." I pointed and took another step forward.

The door was calling to me, but Asher grabbed my arm.

"You see a door?" he asked slowly. "It's the door to Faery."

"But why can't you see it?" I frowned and stepped closer to the buzzing magic.

"Aurelia, I wouldn't get too close," he warned just as the magic wavered.

A gloved hand reached out of the door and latched onto my arm. I screamed as I was pulled through the misty door and into oblivion.

CHAPTER 2
GREY

I spun on the half-Fae. "What the fuck are you doing here?"

Dan's face had paled as realization dawned on him. What the fuck was he thinking, coming down here when he knew Aurelia would be here? I wrapped my hand around his throat and lifted him to his toes. His brown eyes widened as I cut off his airway.

"You better have a real good reason for being here right now." I shook him roughly.

How dare he defy me?

He's fucking ruined everything, and now my mate wants nothing to do with me. I should kill him.

My wolf growled his agreement in my mind.

Kill. Kill. Kill.

The fact my wolf was so on board with killing Dan was seriously concerning, but I still had use for the Fae. I dropped him roughly to the ground and he stumbled back.

"The artifact." Dan coughed as he bent over, trying to take in huge gulps of air.

"What about the artifact?" I snapped.

Why would he bring that up? Especially since I no longer needed it. Aurelia had changed everything. I just had to figure out how to get her back.

"It's being moved," he croaked.

"Does it even fucking matter now? Idiot. You drove away the only person who could have retrieved it!" I bellowed.

I threw my hands up and spun away before I did more than simply choke the moron. How could he be so stupid?

Catching movement from the corner of my eye, I grinned as Karma tried to slink away. "Where do you think you're going?" I growled.

I stormed around the ring, careful not to cross the barrier. Zeke, one of the riders, was a master when it came to nasty little enchantments, and I wouldn't venture inside the ring until he removed it.

He wrenched Karma back with his big hand on her arm and pulled her into his chest.

"Where are you going, little witch?" Zeke grinned.

Karma thrashed against him as I prowled over to her.

"Did you think you would get out of being punished?" I grinned maliciously.

"It was all Layla," she replied through gritted teeth as she continued to thrash against Zeke's hold on her.

"We already told you there's no way that's possible, so give it a rest. Your voice is giving me a headache," I said dismissively.

"I didn't do this, boss. You can't kill me. Please! I didn't betray you," Karma wailed as Zeke dragged her to the elevator.

"Put her in the cells, I need to go after my mate," I growled and stepped up to my private elevator.

I stabbed at the button until the doors opened.

Dan stepped in next to me and I raised an eyebrow. "Where do you think you're going?"

"It's my fault Aurelia is gone, and I'm going to help you find her." He crossed his arms over his chest.

"You really think I'm going to let you near my mate when I'm trying to get her back?" I barked.

"I'm the best tracker you have," he reminded me as the elevator doors closed and the car started to move.

He wasn't wrong, but he'd also failed to track down my mate in the beginning. It was probably for the best or I wouldn't have had the time that I did with her.

"You caused this, and she would kill you rather than go anywhere with you." I shook my head and ran a hand through my messy black hair.

It wasn't the pristine style I normally wore because I'd run my fingers through it repeatedly since Aurelia left.

"I caused this problem, as you said. I will take the princess' wrath. She is Fae royalty, and I am half-Fae. I have just as much loyalty to her as I do to you," Dan said solemnly.

"Just like that?" I asked, shocked.

He finds out she's the princess of the realm that threw him out and he's suddenly loyal to her? What the fuck?

I threw my hands up. "Fine, but don't cry to me if she beats you to a fucking pulp and uses you for magical target practice." I shook my head.

The elevator dinged and the doors slid open to reveal the lobby of the facility. All was quiet in the large, open floorplan office.

The reception desk was empty. The receptionist was probably still downstairs waiting for an elevator to bring her up and back to work.

My shoes squeaked on the tile floor as we raced to the front doors. The sun was too bright and made me wince.

I scanned the area and groaned. "Fuck. Asher's motorcycle is gone."

Where was he taking her and what the hell was he playing at here? I pulled my phone from my pocket and called the rider, but his number rang out to voicemail.

"He'd better not be trying to poach my mate. I will gut the motherfucker. I don't care who he is." I gripped my phone tighter.

"Asher would never. He's probably just giving her the space she needs while keeping her safe." Dan clapped me on the shoulder.

He was right, of course. Asher wouldn't get in between a mate bond. He was probably protecting her.

"Let's go after them." I jogged to the car I'd left out front for a quick getaway.

We jumped in and took the dirt road at high speed. They couldn't be too far away yet.

"Keep an eye out for anything suspicious, just in case. I wouldn't put it past Malcolm to try something else," I said, never taking my eyes off the road.

"What is that?" Dan pointed to something in the middle of the road, just on the other side.

Orange embers danced off gleaming metal and I cursed. The black insignia of the hunt gleamed under the flames.

"That fire is really close to the gas tank." Dan warned.

"That's Asher's bike. Where the fuck are they?" I asked as I cut the engine and slammed open the door.

"Boss, I don't think it's a good idea to get any closer."

"I need to make sure my mate isn't trapped under the fucking motorcycle." I raced to the edge of the ward, but the heat flared and ignited the gas tank. A deafening boom filled the air as I leapt away and into the forest and behind a tree.

Twisted metal rained down onto the dirt road in a hail of flames and ash.

"Grey!" Dan called out from the other side of the inferno. "Are you okay, boss?"

"I'm fine. I'm going to search the woods. I don't think they were here," I called back and turn to the forest.

Shifting was the most effective way to track my mate's scent. My wolf would have known her scent anywhere but with him wanting to tear Dan's throat out, I wasn't sure that was the best idea.

The faint scent of lilacs and smoke hit me, and my wolf whined in my head. He had a better nose than I ever would, so with little choice in the matter, I stripped my suit off and shifted.

I took off bounding through the trees, my mate's fading scent stronger than it had been in while I was in my human form.

What the hell happened? How did they crash just outside the wards?

Asher was a rider of the damn hunt. He could drive or ride anything on wheels with speed and accuracy, so why was his bike sitting in pieces in the middle of the road?

My ears drew back as another scent filled my snout. Asher was following behind her by at least a couple minutes. His scent was a bit stronger than Aurelia's.

The trees swayed in the cool breeze and blew some of her scent away. If I wasn't careful, I would end up lost and running in circles.

I continued moving in the same direction for a long time with no trace of my mate except the faint scent of lilacs and Asher's musky scent tinged with magic.

Where were they going? The trail just kept moving deeper into the forest. Had someone been chasing them?

Did they have a confrontation with Malcolm at the wards? Malcolm was a pureblood Fae, and he surely could have gotten past my wards, right? So, if it was him, then why did he wait until they were outside to strike?

A twig snapped and my wolf snarled at the possible threat.

Who the hell thought it was a good idea to sneak up on the shifter king?

I growled low in my throat but whoever was coming toward me was moving fast and clumsily through the forest.

There was no way it was anyone trained by the facility. They would know to be stealthy no matter how fast they were moving. They wanted me to know they were coming, or they weren't trained correctly. Either way, my hackles were up. I crouched low, ready to pounce.

Ten feet to my left, Dan crashed through the trees. I growled, low and menacing. The idiot was louder than a herd of elephants.

My wolf lunged at him, snarling a warning, and Dan held his hands up in surrender. "Easy, boss. I'm here to help."

My wolf snarled again. The man was the reason my mate had left me, and he still wanted to tear him apart.

Easy, I tried to calm my wolf. *He's a friend and trying to help.*

My wolf snarled one more time. He didn't want Dan anywhere near our mate after he'd shot her with a dart. I didn't blame him, but we needed his help.

My wolf relaxed but growled when Dan got too close.

"I brought your clothes," Dan said.

He pulled a bag over his shoulder and dropped it on the ground in front of me.

I shook my head and picked the bag up off the ground with my teeth and bounded forward again. Her scent was growing colder as I ran through the woods with Dan hot on my heels.

I broke through the trees into a large clearing. The scent of my mate dissipated on the breeze and my wolf growled angrily.

He sniffed at the ground as he trotted around the clearing until the spicy scent of Fae magic filled the air.

My human self took over my body once more and I quickly shifted, dropping the bag at my feet. Crouching low in my human skin, I opened the duffle and dug through it, dressing quickly and scanning the clearing.

"There's something here," I said.

Magic tingled against my skin even though I couldn't see anything. I circled the entire clearing but there was no scent of my mate.

Her trail had gone cold.

She was gone and wherever she went, Asher was with her.

CHAPTER 3
AURELIA

I screamed into the void. The hand around my arm was bruising my skin and I wanted to be released.

I was suspended within time and space. Then a sucking sound became loud in my ears, and I fell in a heap on soft, vibrant, green grass.

"What the fuck?" I growled, pressing my fingers into the lush ground.

Sitting up, I scanned my surroundings.

Where the fuck am I?

The trees were different—prettier, somehow. They were a brighter green than anything I'd ever seen before.

Asher groaned from the where he was on the ground next to me. His hand was on my arm. "Are we..."

"Are we what?" I frowned.

"I haven't seen colors this bright in centuries," Asher said with awe, slowly sitting up and looking around as I was.

"What do you mean? Where are we, Asher?" I chewed my lip.

A gloved hand thrust in my face, and I reared back.

"Who the fuck are you?" I asked, peering up at the man.

His blond brows drew down as he cocked his head to the side.

"Princess Aurelia, do you not remember me? I have been searching for you for years." He crouched in front of me with a frown on his strangely pleasant face.

Asher tensed beside me. "How am I here?"

"Our princess willed it," the man said softly. "I just want to know why."

"Oh, I don't know. A strange hand grabbed me through a magical door, and I didn't want to get dragged into yet another kidnapping situation." I glared at the stranger. "Now, who are you and where am I?"

"My apologies, Princess Aurelia. My name is Fenrick. I was your personal guard as a child. I have been searching for you for years." Fenrick grinned as though he'd won the lottery and while he must have felt like he had, I certainly hadn't.

"Where am I?" I asked again, softly this time.

Shit. Did we get dragged into Faery? How is that possible?

I turned to Asher, who was glancing around the space in awe.

"You're home. Finally." Fenrick grinned.

He held his hand out to me again, but I peered at Asher. I could trust him more than this weird guy above us.

"I'm in Faery?" I asked the giant beside me, who nodded.

Shit.

"I was banned just like everyone else," Asher whispered. "How?"

Fenrick huffed out a breath. "Like I said, you are here because our princess willed it so. She has the ability to close our realm forever or open it up to the witches, shifters and half-bloods to return."

"Wait, what? I thought there was something I had to do. The book." I jumped to my feet, my heart pounding.

"You just have to will it, Princess Aurelia. It's why you were taken away. The elders will not be kind to you," Fenrick said.

I just had to will it? Was he serious?

"Then why did you bring her back here?" Asher threw his hands up in exasperation.

I waved a hand at Asher. "It's fine. I know about the threat of the elders, but if they're a danger and you were my protector, why am I here?"

"Malcolm. He was never supposed to abduct you as a child. I have been tasked by your parents to bring you back to them." Fenrick ran a hand over his head.

"He said I was his. What did he mean by that?"

I did not belong to him or anyone else. The Fae was deranged.

Fenrick frowned, the expression in his eyes guilty. "You were betrothed to the captain of the king's guard as a baby. There is a connection between you."

I jumped to my feet. "What does that mean? Is that why he keeps finding me?"

Fenrick closed his eyes and sighed. He didn't want to tell me what I feared. I would never escape Malcolm completely.

Asher ran a hand through his hair. "Well, does he know where we are?"

"No, not right now, he doesn't, and it will be a while before he thinks to look in Faery," Fenrick said.

"How does the princess even know she can trust you? She has no memories of this place." Asher crossed his arms over his chest and glared at the blond man.

I was glad for the rider's overprotective instincts.

Fenrick didn't seem fazed at all as he shrugged. "I was tasked with bringing the princess home and keeping her safe. If Malcolm has become a danger to her, then I will deal with him."

"That doesn't answer my question," Asher growled.

"What do you want from me, rider? Do you want an oath?" Fenrick stepped into Asher's space.

Were they about to fight? What the hell was even happening here?

"Would you even be able to keep that oath? What happens if your elders order you to kill her or bring her to them? You can't disobey them and then your oath would kill you anyway!" Asher yelled.

Fenrick sighed. He glanced away and took a step away from Asher.

"He's right, isn't he?" I asked. "The Fae will do anything to keep the others out of Faery."

I shook my head in disgust. The more I learned of the Fae, the more I despised them. They were my people, but they also were a bunch of privileged monsters.

"C'mon, Princess, we need to find a way back to the human realm. It's not safe for you inside Faery," Asher said and held out a hand to me.

"Am I safe anywhere? This is too fucking much. I don't want to be the one everyone craves to control. I don't want to be the reason why people never get to go back to their homes." I threw my hands up.

I spun around at the sound of a twig snapping. Magic filled my palms as several Fae in gleaming silver armor and purple crests across the chest marched into the room.

"What is this?" I asked Fenrick as the guards surrounded us.

"We had a feeling after all these years that you would not be amenable to coming to the palace and took... precautions." Fenrick lowered his gaze to the ground.

"I knew we couldn't trust you," Asher said in a lethal whisper.

One of the soldiers stepped forward with a sneer. "You brought a rider of the hunt through the portal?"

He glared at me through the thin slits of his medieval-style helmet.

"Yes, I brought him through the portal with me. So?" I squared my shoulders, refusing to back down.

"He's a dangerous criminal." The soldier unsheathed his sword, pointing it at Asher.

"Yeah, and he's the only person that has never lied to me or tried to use me for his own plans." I raised an eyebrow at Fenrick.

He lowered his eyes in shame, but he would do it again in a second if he was ordered to. I needed to remember that I couldn't trust anyone in this world or any other.

"Honestly," Asher chuckled. "You needed ten of the king's men to bring in a tiny princess?"

Swords unsheathed all around us, pointing at Asher.

"We will not be disrespected by someone who was banished along with the other undesirables." The soldier angrily poked Asher with the tip of his blade.

Fenrick stepped in front of me and waved the weapons away. "Come with us, Princess Aurelia."

He held his hand out to me and I eyed it like a snake about to strike.

"You act like I have a choice," I growled, waving at all the soldiers ready to take me in by force.

"I would much rather you come willingly," Fenrick huffed. "But when we were alerted to your presence, the king and queen ordered us to bring you in safely by any means necessary."

"Let's go, then." I waved for him to lead.

The nameless soldier stepped in closer to Asher and got right in his face. "Detain him until he can be expelled from the realm again."

"What?" I yelled. "You can't."

"He's not supposed to be here, Princess Aurelia, and your parents will agree. He needs to be detained." The man glared at me.

Asher stood there unmoving. He didn't struggle at all. The

soldiers wrapped some kind of metal cuffs around his wrists behind his back and Asher flinched when they clicked shut.

"I don't care what you all think of him. I brought him here and I want him to stay with me." I let magic crackle against my palms again, ready for a fight.

Fenrick ran a palm down his face. "The king and queen will decide what to do with him."

"This is bullshit!" I yelled.

My magic grew stronger and ran up my arms. My wings beat angrily behind my back as I glared at all the soldiers surrounding us.

Asher stiffened. "Princess, it's okay, I'm fine. Calm down," he said softly.

"You realize that is not the way to get me to calm down, right?" I asked through gritted teeth.

"Breathe with me," Asher said in a soothing voice.

I wasn't scared this time though, I was angry.

How dare they pull me from the forest and then demand that I let them take my friend from me.

It was bullshit.

"Princess, regain control," Asher said with warning in his tone.

"I don't want to," I growled.

The soldiers stepped away from me, glancing between each other warily.

They should be worried. I'm done letting assholes push me around. I'm over it.

"Aurelia!" Asher shouted.

I glanced over to him, and his eyes held worry as well.

"They don't get to boss me around and bully me into being who and what they want me to be." I held my hand out in front of me, about to unleash the magic.

"Stop!" Fenrick shouted. "Let him go. We will take him in with the princess."

The nameless soldier sneered at us, not liking the idea at all, but he nodded to the guards behind Asher, and they quickly released him.

I let the magic fizzle out and grinned. "Lead the way to the castle, Fenrick."

The guard eyed me warily as Asher stepped up beside me.

"Are you okay, Aurelia?" my protector whispered.

"No, I really am not okay. This is just one more thing to add on to this shit day." I shook my head and followed Fenrick.

"It will be fine as long as we figure something out," he said mostly to himself.

He didn't want to be here without his brothers. I knew how close they were. I'd seen it firsthand. We needed to get out of this realm and back to our lives, but where would that leave me when we did?

The mark from Grey's bite tingled on my shoulder and anger bubbled up inside me. Violet magic crackled in my palms. His betrayal was the most pain I'd ever felt in my life. It was worse than freezing and starving in that dirty alley as a child.

as we trudged through the forest in silence, I was lost in thought. The soldiers still surrounded us, but I ignored them. We broke through the tree line onto a manicured lawn. A gleaming white castle towered above me.

Memories flashed in my mind so quickly that I couldn't quite catch them. The only one that I could grasp was the fleeting glimpse of that castle over Malcolm's shoulder as he abducted me and took me away.

I'd lived in this castle as a child. I was now sure of it. It was one more thing that proved I was who everyone said I was, damnit.

Am I the only girl in history who doesn't want to be a princess?

"Princess," Fenrick said softly and put his hand on the small of my back.

Asher growled at the gesture, but I cut him off.

"What, Fenrick?" I sighed and stepped sideways, away from his hand.

Fenrick let his hand drop to his side and turned to the castle looming ahead.

I froze. What would I find when I went inside? Did I care?

"Welcome home, Princess Aurelia," Fenrick said, and led the way inside.

This wasn't my home. I had no home, and I probably never would.

CHAPTER 4
GREY

I slammed my phone down on the desk. "Where the fuck is Asher?"

Zeke sat back in his chair and ran a hand down his beard in thought. "We can't connect with him at all. It's like he's in another realm."

My jaw dropped. "You don't think?" I asked, my brows rising in surprise.

That's not possible. No one has been able to find the portal. No one has been able to get to Faery in centuries.

"He's not dead," Zeke growled. He clenched his hand into a tight fist on the arm of the chair.

"I never said he was dead, I was asking if it's possible that he could be off world." I scrubbed a hand over my face.

Stubble lined my jaw. I hadn't done much of anything but search for Aurelia since she disappeared.

"How? We were all banished." Zeke shook his head.

"Malcolm abducted Aurelia because she could close off Faery from us. What if she's also able to bring people home?" I asked and flopped back in my chair.

"I have an idea." Zeke sat forward with his elbows resting on his knees.

Fiona buzzed into the room carrying a plate with her magic and set it on the desk between us.

"What idea?" I frowned.

"Her." He pointed at Fiona. "The sub-Fae weren't banished."

"Motherfucker!" I shouted.

Why the fuck had I never thought of that? We couldn't see the portal because we were banished but the sub-Fae could probably see it.

"We need to go to the place where they disappeared." Zeke stood from the chair.

"What good will that do us, though?" I asked.

Sure, we would know where the portal was and where to find Aurelia, but we wouldn't be able to actually find them. We couldn't go into the portal.

"The sprite can find her and get Ash a message." Zeke shrugged and made his way to the door to my office.

Fiona glowed green with excitement. "You want me to find Miss Aurelia?"

"You think you can do that?" Zeke grinned.

Fiona fluttered excitedly. "If I can see the portal, I will go find the mistress."

I wasn't so sure about this, but it was the best option we had. If Malcolm had her, I was going to find a way to my mate and kill the bastard, even if she didn't want anything to do with me.

"Let's go back to the facility then." I stood from my chair and grabbed my keys.

I stormed through the penthouse and to the elevator then stabbed at the button.

"You think this will work?" Fiona asked softly from her place fluttering in front of me.

"I think it's our best shot." I stepped into the elevator with the others following behind me.

Fiona landed lightly on my shoulder as we rode the elevator down.

"I don't think Malcolm has her," Zeke said suddenly.

"What do you mean?" I asked as the elevator dinged.

I stepped out into the underground garage. Zeke was quiet for a moment before he answered, "He wouldn't have taken Asher as well. How the hell did Asher even get through? Nothing makes sense." He shook his head before opening the passenger door of the car.

"I don't know yet." I slammed the door behind me and started the engine.

Did Aurelia unknowingly hop into Faery and take Asher with her? How could she possibly do that?

There was a prophecy saying that she would either close Faery or open it back up, but I'd thought she would need the book to do that. Could she do it on her own?

The drive to the facility was silent. I was in my head, wishing my mate would return. Could she come back? Did someone other than Malcolm abduct her this time?

I pulled off the dirt road just outside the wards where Asher's motorcycle exploded. Fiona fluttered out of the car before I could get out.

"What is that?" she asked.

She cocked her head to the side as she buzzed to the trees.

"Fiona, slow down!" I yelled.

I picked my way through the trees and underbrush much slower in my human form than my wolf had only days ago.

Zeke kept pace beside me, staring at Fiona as she buzzed through the forest.

The trees swayed in the breeze, ruffling them all in the direction Fiona was flying.

"What the hell is happening?" I stared at the tops of the trees.

Zeke turned, peering at me. "What are you talking about?"

"The trees." I frowned.

He turned his gaze up to the trees and his eyes widened. "Are they showing her the way?"

"They aren't Fae trees. They aren't alive in the same way as the Fae trees." I shook my head.

There was no way they were actually pointing us in the direction of the portal, right?

"That makes me think the portal could actually have been here the whole time." Zeke pushed a branch away.

We broke through the tree line into the clearing, where Fiona buzzed around excitedly.

"Do you see anything?" I asked Zeke.

He shook his head. "Nothing."

"What do you mean?" Fiona asked, turning to us and back to something only she could see.

"It's an empty clearing," I said.

My wolf perked up and growled in my head. Could he sense something in the clearing I couldn't see?

"There's a shimmering purple door," Fiona scoffed.

"Where?" I stepped forward.

Could I push through the portal even if I couldn't see it? To my knowledge, no one had ever tried.

Fiona fluttered a few feet away and pointed at empty space. She glanced back at us, exasperated when we shrugged.

Zeke ran a hand over his hair. "So, there is a portal there that we can't see, and you just so happened to buy the land it's on."

"Why do I feel like this is too much of a coincidence?" I circled the space Fiona pointed to.

"You said there was a prophecy, right?" Zeke stared at the empty space.

"Yeah," I said slowly.

What was he getting at? Was he saying that whatever this prophecy was, I was a part of it?

"The fates are crazy bitches. I wouldn't put anything past them." Zeke took a step forward and frowned.

He strolled confidently to the spot that Fiona indicated, and a buzzing filled the air before he cursed and his body flew back ten feet.

"Fuck, are you okay?" I asked as I rushed to him.

"There's some kind of ward there or something." Zeke groaned then slowly sat up and shook his head to clear it.

Fiona's tinkling giggle filled the space. "You can't just walk through a closed door, silly."

"You could have warned me," Zeke grumbled and rubbed his forehead.

"Oops, I forgot you can't see it." Fiona fluttered closer to Zeke.

The rider bared his teeth at her.

"Back off, Zeke," I warned.

No one threatened the sprites. They were under my protection, and Zeke knew that better than anyone.

Zeke shook his head and picked himself up off the ground, dusted himself off and moved to the invisible portal.

"Can you open the door?" Zeke asked over his shoulder.

"I'm not sure." Fiona frowned and buzzed to the door.

"I don't know if that's a good idea. What if you can't get back?" I rubbed my neck.

"Well, I think we give her a message first, just in case she can't get back." Zeke shrugged.

"You send the message to Ash," I said, stepping away.

My mate wouldn't listen to a message from me. She would probably just stay in Faery to spite me.

"She may not be as upset now, friend." Zeke clapped me on the shoulder.

"It's only been a couple days. We have no idea what's happening to her right now." I shook my head.

"Fine. Fiona, tell Ash that we are looking for him if you can't get back. Find out what is happening with them and try to get back to us as quickly as possible."

"I will get any information I can and report back," Fiona said with a nod.

Her determination shone in her tiny eyes. She was not going to let us down. She loved Aurelia just as much as I did. Well... almost.

Why the fuck did I lie to her in the first place? I should have told her about Dan and that we were investigating the witch's death from the beginning.

Fiona buzzed closer to the spot where she indicated the portal was and took one last, long glance at me before flying into the space and disappearing with a pop.

"She was able to get in," Zeke said, shocked.

I hadn't been entirely sure she would be able to get in there either.

I don't know how this could help our situation. For all I knew, she liked it there and never wanted to come back to a place where she felt she'd never belonged.

"Let's see if she can get back before we start celebrating," I said.

I ran a hand through my mussed hair and pulled my phone out of my pocket.

Dan picked up on the second ring. "Yeah, boss?" His voice was wary.

"I need you to come out to the clearing with our best guards. I want this place guarded around the clock." I huffed out a breath.

"Do you want the trolls?" he asked.

I frowned as something occurred to me. Could the trolls see

the portal? I didn't remember if the trolls were expelled with us or if they left persecution before we were banished.

"Just bring one troll for now, I need to test a theory." I glanced up at Zeke's gasp.

"On it, boss." Dan said, and I hung up the phone.

"I don't think they'll be able to see it," Zeke said quietly.

I wandered over to the nearest tree and sat with my back resting against it. "I don't know. I can't remember if they were expelled."

"Everyone would know that the portal was here if the trolls could cross over." Zeke sat down next to me with his knee bent and his elbow resting on it.

"People overlook the trolls. I'm guilty of doing the same. No one would think to ask them if they can sense a portal since they are notoriously private creatures." I clenched my fists.

I could have had a way in, or to at least get goods out of Faery this whole time. It pissed me off that I'd been so stupid not to hire trolls and sprites to search for the portal.

We sat in silence for a long time as we waited for Dan to come out with the troll. It would take a while. I watched the portal, waiting for Fiona as well. Would she be able to get back?

Did I just force her to get stuck in Faery with no possible escape?

I leaned my head back against the tree and closed my eyes tightly. Freya was going to kill me or leave me forever if anything happened to Fiona. If she found out that her sister was stuck in Faery with no way to return to her, Freya would search for the portal and go find her.

They were inseparable. This would not go over well.

The ground rumbled beneath me. I stood and turned in the direction of the facility.

Dan broke the tree line first, followed by a huge troll.

The troll gasped loudly, "What is that?"

"You can see it?" I asked, taking a step toward the troll.

"It's the door to Faery. Why did you bring me here?" The ground rumbled as he took a step back.

A light buzzing filled the air, and something flew by my head frantically.

"Fiona?" I asked, my eyes wide with shock.

She was frazzled and speeding all around the clearing. How did she manage to get that freaked out? She had only been gone a matter of minutes.

"Master Grey?" she asked in shock. "You're still here?"

"What do you mean? You've only been gone about an hour," I said slowly.

That same buzzing filled the air and Fiona's eyes widened again. "Something's coming through."

I widened my stance and waited as magic pulsed in the air.

A large body flew toward me, and I cursed.

Zeke lunged forward to grab the body. "Ash? What the fuck did they do to you?"

"Where's Aurelia?" I asked warily, watching the empty space where the portal was supposed to be.

"She's gone," a knight of the shadow court said as he appeared out of thin air. "And she's never coming back."

CHAPTER 5
Aurelia

I dragged my feet as we made our way through the castle. "Where are you taking us?"

Fenrick was leading the way, and I scowled at him. He'd tried to get me to trust him when he'd been planning on ambushing me from the beginning.

Fenrick glanced at me over his shoulder. "The king and queen have requested to see you in the throne room."

"And what if I don't care?" I asked snidely. I didn't care. I wasn't holding anything back from these people.

"Princess." Fenrick blew out an aggravated breath.

"Just take me to them and then let me go. I didn't ask to be here." I held my chin up high.

Everyone wanted a piece of me, but no one actually wanted to treat me with any kind of respect or cared enough not to betray me.

Grey.

I shook my head, clearing it of any thoughts of the traitorous shifter. He'd only wanted me for a job. He'd caused all my problems from the beginning, sending that man after me and then pretending he had no idea.

Large, gilded doors stood before me as Fenrick stopped. I glanced at Asher next to me and he shot me an encouraging smile.

"You can do this. Show them the princess you are," Asher whispered.

I rolled my shoulders back and held my head high. I raised my chin in the air as Fenrick nodded to the guards on either side of the door and they opened them.

The room was huge, even bigger than Grey's penthouse. I hated that I compared everything to him.

The room was done in silver and a deep royal purple. There was a raised dais in the middle of the space with two huge seats in the middle.

The room had memories flashing in my mind. Seats filled the space while I sat in a smaller chair in a tulle-covered monstrosity as the king and queen held court. Malcolm stood on one side of my father and Fenrick stood behind me.

Huh? So, he hadn't been lying about being my protector but he still had to answer to the king and queen, which made him suspect until I could prove otherwise.

Shaking my head, I attempted to clear it of the weird memories. I didn't want to have reminders of this place and these people, but I did. And they were getting clearer by the minute.

I peered at the people on the thrones, both just as regal as I remembered. The queen had white-blonde hair just like me, but her eyes were a deep green.

The man had caramel-colored hair, but his sky-blue eyes matched mine. These were definitely my parents. If only I could remember what kind of people they were.

"Aurelia?" the woman gasped as she stood from her throne.

I stiffened as she moved toward me with a hand covering her mouth.

"Yes, that's me." I glanced away.

"You truly don't remember us?" she asked softly.

She was elegant and looked way too young to be my mother. Her deep purple dress was bell-shaped but hugged her trim waist. Her skin was flawless.

"I remember a little bit but not much." I shook my head and held my ground even though she moved into my space.

"You are even more beautiful than I imagined you would be." The queen smiled.

She put a hand to my cheek and swiped her thumb across my cheekbone. "How are you here?"

"Your man, Fenrick, pulled me through a portal. Oh, wait. Can't forget Malcolm abducted me too and was not kind. He hurt my friends." I kept my gaze straight ahead.

If I looked into her sad eyes, I would break. I couldn't do that. They gave the order to bring me back against my will.

I understood that they missed their daughter, but I had very few memories of them, and it wasn't fair of them to put their issues with my abduction on me.

"Aurelia, what did Malcolm do to you?" the king asked.

Asher fidgeted by my side, but I held strong and kept my chin up. "He abducted me and then when I tried to escape, he injured me and locked me in a basement."

The queen gasped, bringing her fingers to her lips again. "Surely, Malcolm would never hurt you. He's your betrothed."

"You mean you tied us together when I was a child without my consent, and when he didn't get what he was told was his, he lashed out." I shook my head and stepped away from the woman.

"Aurelia," the king said in warning. "You will not speak to your mother like that."

"My mother? The only mother I remember was murdered by Malcolm and I was left to take the fall," I growled back.

The king sat forward on his throne at the same time the guards stepped forward. The king held up a hand indicating to the guards they needed to stop.

"I did not know that Malcolm had stooped so low." The king sighed.

"Well, how could you? He stayed in the human realm and waited for the right time to abduct me again." I shook my head.

"What happened to you, my daughter?" the queen asked.

"I don't think there is enough time in this visit to tell you both everything that happened to me since the first time I was abducted." I shrugged.

"We have plenty of time to learn all the things about each other now that you are back." The queen smiled.

"What do you mean by that?" I asked, stepping back away from the queen and bumping into Fenrick.

"Well, you are home now. We have plenty of time to catch up." The queen frowned.

"I can't stay. I have to stop Malcolm. He will find me and try to force me to close off the portal." I shook my head.

"My queen," Fenrick said with a bow. "She has been affected by the supernaturals in Earth realm."

The queen gasped and the king turned angry eyes on me. "What do you mean? You wish to let them return to our realm?"

"Do you know what they've gone through the past few centuries?" I asked angrily. "They have to hide what they are from the humans. They are miserable and all because Fae are racist."

"So?" the king thundered. "They do not belong here. They were banished for a reason."

Asher stepped forward, glaring at the king. "We did nothing to deserve being sent away."

"You say you don't deserve to be banished even though you were one of the worst of those we got rid of," the king spat.

"How is that?" I shrieked and stepped in front of Asher.

"The riders of the wild hunt are older than time, Aurelia. They cannot be trusted. Step away from him." My mother held her hand out to me, beckoning me forward.

I glanced at Asher out of the corner of my eye, but his expression gave nothing away.

"I don't care. He has been kinder to me than anyone else in my entire life." I crossed my arms over my chest.

"You will learn to care!" the king boomed. "You don't get to be a petulant child."

"A petulant child?" I bellowed. "I have never been a spoiled child that I remember. My friends don't deserve the fate they were saddled with."

"And what fate is that?" the queen asked. Tears rimmed her eyes but she didn't let them fall.

I felt badly for her. She'd lost her child, then I lost my memory and had ties to other supernaturals they were supposed to hate. What Malcolm and the elders did to all of us wasn't fair.

"A fate that made them hide from the humans and not permit their true nature to run free in that realm. They have been suffering for centuries, and Malcolm nearly beat me to death to get me to block them from ever going home." I shook my head.

"Why do they have to hide?" the queen asked.

Asher stepped forward and bowed his head. "The shifters cannot shift openly. If they did, they would be hunted by the human authorities and experimented on. The witches? They already knew the humans would fear them from the time of the witch trials."

Asher shook his head, glaring at the king and queen with disgust.

"That sounds terrible," the queen gasped. "The elders couldn't have known that would happen. Right?"

"Are you really that naïve, your majesty?" Asher raised a brow.

I turned to Asher with wide eyes. That was rude. I peered at my parents, but neither seemed to be angry at his comment.

"Asher," I warned.

"No, the elders knew exactly what they were doing to the rest of us. They knew we would suffer as they have their own seers, which is why they received the prophecy in the first place." Asher shook his head.

"Asher," I tried to warn again.

"It's okay, Aurelia," the queen whispered. "We need to know what those old bastards planned."

I burst into a fit of laughter at the regal queen and her curse words.

"Mother, what was that?" I asked in a shocked gasp.

Her eyes widened and happiness shone inside her eyes. "I am angry the elders think they can harm people at will, but so happy you recognize me as your mother."

"Wait, what?" I asked, shocked.

"Those old bastards have no idea what they are doing and even if they did, we can't let them get away with it, Channing," my mother said and glared up at the king.

I took a step back. What the hell was going on here? Were my parents agreeing with me about the ban on the other supernaturals.

"Are you serious?" I scanned the throne room. "You don't agree with them?"

"No," my mother growled. "They are a bunch of old fools."

"Katrina!" my father bellowed. "You cannot speak such things."

The queen scowled at him but kept her mouth shut. A commotion sounded from outside the throne room, and I groaned. What the hell was going on? Was something happening outside?

"Who's there?" the king hollered.

The doors to the throne room flew open and five old men stormed in with a dozen guards.

"What is the meaning of this?" my mother screamed.

She waved her hand and the knights around the room all unsheathed their swords, pointing them at the new arrivals.

A man with a cane pushed through the crowd into the throne room. His beady eyes narrowed on me.

"Queen Katrina, why have you not told us of your daughter's return?" the man demanded.

"She's only just returned," the queen scoffed. "What difference does it make to you?"

The king stood from his throne and moved to stand between me and the men.

Are these the elders? Are they a threat to me?

I glanced at Asher, who immediately stiffened.

So, they are a threat. That's good to know.

The man with the beady eyes glared at me before turning his focus on Asher. "I think it is of the utmost importance to us. Especially since she brought a rider of the hunt with her."

The old men gasped and started screaming obscenities.

One man shouted over the rest, "Abominations aren't permitted here. I told you we should have taken care of her as a child!"

"And by take care of her, you mean murder an innocent child?" Asher sneered. "You call us the abominations."

"Asher," I warned, widening my eyes at my defender. He didn't need to be bringing more attention to himself than there already was. What was he thinking?

"Eliminate the threat to our very way of life is what I meant," the loudmouth barked back at him.

Fenrick stiffened beside me and clenched the sword tighter in his fist.

Is he expecting a fight?

"That threat is my daughter!" King Channing roared.

All the knights stiffened at the king's tone.

"How do you know that she hasn't brought more people with her?" Beady-eyed guy asked, smacking his cane on the marble floor.

Fenrick stepped forward. "I pulled her through the portal and in her fear, she dragged the rider with her."

It wasn't lost on me that he stepped right in front of me, blocking me from the elders.

"She's coming with us," the beady-eyed man proclaimed just as the doors to the throne room burst open and guards flooded the room.

There are too many of them. What the hell are we going to do?

CHAPTER 6
GREY

"What do you mean?" I growled. My hands shifted to claws as I stared down the shadow Fae. He was asking to get murdered unless he told me what happened to my friend and my mate.

"The elders have her," he said.

"The elders?" I asked.

Shit. That was the worst possible thing that could happen. We needed to get her out of there. Fast.

"I have been tasked to find Malcolm," the shadow Fae informed.

"If I find that bastard, I'm going to gut him for this." I ran a hand through my hair.

"I don't think you will. He has stolen a priceless artifact from our princess, and it may be the only thing that can save her from the elders. We need Malcolm alive." The man sheathed his sword.

Dan stepped forward. "Are you talking about the book?"

"Yes, how do you know of it?" The shadow Fae's tone was filled with loathing.

Dan was half-Fae and half-human, and the pureblood

assholes didn't like their bloodlines being tainted with other species.

It was one of the reasons we were all banished.

"I saw him take it with the help of a spell." Dan crossed his arms over his chest.

He wasn't taking the knight's shit. Good.

"We need that book if we are to fulfill the prophecy and you are to be allowed into Faery." The man removed his gloves. "It's an honor to meet you, shifter king. My name is Fenrick."

I reached out and shook the Fae's hand. "Please, call me Grey. I don't advertise that I am the king of shifters. I don't want to until I can get my people home."

"That's admirable. The elders will go to great lengths to make sure that never happens." Fenrick shook his head.

"Why would you help me with this then?" I asked.

It didn't make any sense. Why would the Fae help us? The elders banished us, but it looked like the shadow court wanted my help.

"Our princess has been threatened and the king and queen are rethinking the decision to banish you all." Fenrick shrugged.

Asher groaned and writhed on the ground. His face was bruised and bloody. What had they done to him?

"Aurelia," he whispered.

"What about Aurelia?" I rushed over and knelt beside him.

One eye was completely swollen shut and blood trailed down his chin from the cut on his lip. He blinked one eye open, but he was dazed.

"How did I get back?" he mumbled, glancing at Zeke.

"I don't know, but you were talking about Aurelia. What happened?" I asked urgently.

Ash's eyes rolled back in his head before he could speak.

"What the hell did they do to him?" I growled, glaring at Fenrick.

"They didn't take kindly to his presence in Faery and retaliated. I got him out as soon as I could. That's not important." Fenrick moved away from the group.

"What is important?" I asked with a snarl. "He's not okay. He's fucking immortal and look at him."

"The most important thing is finding that book and fast, or something terrible will happen to your mate." Fenrick shook his head.

"Fuck. Okay let's get out of here and regroup." I scanned the clearing, looking for Fiona but didn't find her. "Where's Fiona?"

"The sprite has her own part to play. She went back to the princess." Fenrick shrugged and stormed through the tree line.

"Where the fuck are you going?" I shouted at the Fae warrior's back.

"I'm getting out of the forest where anyone could hear our plans!" he yelled back.

"He's not wrong," Zeke growled.

I didn't particularly like the shadow Fae warrior, but he was right about one thing. I turned to the troll.

"Can you guard the portal?" I asked.

"I don't want to be anywhere near the Fae portal, boss."

"That's precisely why I want you to guard the portal. You don't want to go back to Faery, so you can guard the portal and not disappear on me." I clapped him on the shoulder.

"Of course, boss. I will watch it." The troll nodded.

I followed Fenrick from the forest and back to my car. Zeke carried Asher behind us.

I grimaced when I realized that I would be returning to the penthouse without Fiona. Freya was going to lose her shit in the worst way.

Dan clapped me on the shoulder as he sidled up next to me.

"What's that look for?" he asked.

"Freya." I shook my head.

"She's going to be fucking with you until the end of time for this." Dan chuckled.

"You're not wrong," I grumbled.

I was not looking forward to explaining to the sprite what happened with her sister. That was going to be a pain in the ass.

We made it back to the car and I pulled the keys out of my pocket. "Dan, take Zeke and Asher to the facility and get Ash to a healer."

"On it, boss." Dan waved Zeke over to his Range Rover so they could pile in.

I nodded to Fenrick and got in the driver's seat of my car and waited for the Fae.

He grimaced as he sat in the passenger seat.

"You get used to the claustrophobic feeling." I turned the key in the ignition.

"I haven't spent much time in the human realm." Fenrick folded himself into the passenger seat.

"Did you see my mate?" I asked as I flipped around and drove back toward the city.

"I pulled her into Faery. Had I known what would happen, I never would have brought her back." He blew out a breath of frustration.

"You're the reason that she's in this mess?" I growled.

"I had orders from the king and queen. They wanted their daughter back." He never glanced away from the window.

"It didn't matter what she wanted." I was disgusted.

Of course, it didn't. My father never cared much for what I wanted either and we ended up paying the ultimate price for his ego.

"No, it didn't, but they gave birth to her and have been searching for her for decades," Fenrick said.

"Decades?" I asked curiously.

There was no way she had been taken away from them for

decades. She was maybe twenty and had been at least seven when Malcolm abducted her.

"Time works differently in Faery, it seems. We have been looking for her for a lot longer than she has been alive in the human realm," Fenrick grumbled.

"How long has it been since you ripped her out of the human realm?" I asked.

How long had it been for my mate? Weeks? Months? Did she think that everyone here had forgotten about her?

"It had been two weeks when I pushed the rider through the portal." He shook his head.

"Two weeks isn't a terrible timeframe," I admitted.

Hopefully, she knew that I would be coming to save her. I needed her to have faith in that even if she hated me. I refused to be that man again, and if she gave me a second chance, I would never break her trust.

"It is when she was taken by the elders, and we haven't seen her in weeks," Fenrick said softly.

"How can we know that she's okay?" I asked.

"We don't. We can't. The elders have her, and we don't have much time to waste." Fenrick said.

That was not what I wanted to hear. How the hell were we going to find Malcolm?

"I think we need to check Malcolm's house. The place he took her when he abducted her from my penthouse." I turned the car down another dirt road.

"You know where he lives?" Fenrick seemed shocked.

"I doubt he lives there anymore after we rescued Aurelia. It would be too easy for us to catch him if he still stayed there."

"Malcolm is arrogant enough to stay there and not care if the shifter king found him." Fenrick shook of his head.

"You're not wrong on that one. He also might have left some nasty traps for us and returned to Faery." I gripped the steering wheel tighter in my hands until my knuckles were white.

I wanted a piece of the stupid Fae bastard. My wolf was in full agreement.

"That's not possible," Fenrick said. "He can't go back to Faery without the princess."

"Okay, I'm going to need you to explain." I glanced at the Fae warrior from the corner of my eye.

Why the hell would he need Aurelia to get back into Faery?

"When he took the princess from our realm, the king and queen banished him, and even if he does manage to get back into the realm, there is an order to kill on sight."

"So, that bastard is desperate to find her, but he's stuck in the same situation, where he'll never get back?" I chuckled.

It served the stupid bastard right.

We pulled up to the sprawling ranch house and I cut the engine. I'd never wanted to come back to this place but if it helped me get my mate back, then I would do anything at all. I'd cross realms for her and burn everything in my path.

"There still might be some nasty traps inside. He is a sadistic prick." I opened the car door and got out.

"You don't become the head of the king's guard without being a sadist," Fenrick agreed.

The pile of twisted metal was still beneath the tree that landed on the motorcycles. Luckily for all of us, the riders hadn't been overly concerned about their bikes.

The house had an ominous feel to it that made me shiver. No one had been here since that night apparently, as the door was off its hinges when we walked up the path.

"I don't think he's here," Fenrick mumbled.

He scanned the house as he clenched the hilt of his sword.

"No, but we can have a look around and see if he left the book behind." I stepped through the open door.

"I don't believe he would be that stupid," Fenrick said.

A loud click filled the quiet space.

"Fuck. Don't move. I think one of us just sprung a trap." I grimaced and scanned the floor.

The tile under my foot was depressed a quarter inch below the rest and I groaned.

"I triggered the trap. I'm not even sure what it does or what will happen if I move my foot." I turned to glance over to Fenrick, who grimaced.

"I can't sift." He frowned, concentrating, but he stayed in the exact same place.

"Malcolm has wards on the place. He would make it so no one else could sift in his home."

A ticking filled the room, like a clock ticking down the time until the trap sprung whether I moved or not.

"I don't have a choice. I have to move because either way, this trap is going off," I said.

Fenrick nodded and edged out the front door. It was only a few feet away. I could make it before anything happened.

"Three, two, one," I said and bolted for the door.

An inferno of heat blew me from my feet, and I flew outside as a deafening boom hit my ears. I hit the ground with a thud.

My head pounded and my body burned, forcing a scream from my lungs before everything went black.

CHAPTER 7
Aurelia

I gripped the iron chains tugging at the ends. "What the fuck?"

The beady-eyed elder sneered. "They really didn't do much for your attitude."

"Why am I here?" I asked, scanning the cell.

It was dank and smelled of mildew and rot. Why the fuck did they think I deserved to be behind iron bars and locked in chains?

The stone floors were disgusting, and I was pretty sure the hole in the corner was supposed to be a toilet. The conditions weren't fit for an animal let alone a princess of the damn realm.

"We need to test you to see if you have shadow magic," the man said.

The gleam in his eyes was terrifying. Why would he think I had shadow magic? I had never used such magic, nor had I heard of it.

"That's ridiculous," I said. "I've never used such a thing."

"You also have yet to come into your full powers." He shook his head.

What? I haven't come into my powers? They're already terrifying. What will happen when I have my full powers?

"That can't be right." I chewed my lip.

The elder sighed. "Do you remember nothing?"

"Next to nothing." I shrugged.

I wasn't going to let the elitist bastard faze me. He was not important. I needed to get out of here and look for Asher.

Fenrick had gone with him, and I hoped the rider was okay. It was all my fault if something bad happened to him.

Guilt ate at me, making my stomach roil. I hadn't seen either of them in days.

"The Fae do not come into their full powers until their twenty-fifth birthday. Yours is in just a few days' time." He grunted.

What the fuck? I didn't even know when my damn birthday was. That was really depressing.

"So, you are saying I have to be here for a few days so you can test me for magic I have never heard of before? Great." I shifted and the chains clanked together.

"Why do you think your parents' court is the shadow court?" His beady eyes narrowed on me.

"I don't fucking know. I wasn't even aware that's what it was called." I threw my hands up in frustration.

The chains pulled tight and the manacles scraped against my skin. I winced in pain.

Fuck. That hurt.

The beady-eyed elder chuckled at my discomfort.

"Why are you even here telling me all this?" I asked warily.

I thought they wanted me dead. Why was he telling me all this if they just planned to kill me anyway?

"Just letting you know what to expect before we start experimenting." His grin was malicious.

I widened my eyes. They were going to experiment on me?

I did not want to know what they planned to do to me to make this crazy magic surface. I needed to get out of there as soon as possible.

"I don't even want to know what you plan to do to get the magic to surface." I shuddered and took a step back.

"You will know soon enough." He grinned and waved a hand.

Four council soldiers stepped forward and unlocked the cell door.

He wants to do this now? Fuck.

The soldiers strolled into the cell and unhooked the chains from the wall. One man on each side of me grabbed my arms in a bruising grip.

They shoved me forward and I stumbled slightly. The tight grip on my arms was the only thing that stopped my fall.

They were not being kind or gentle. I ripped away from the man on the right and he sneered as he shoved me forward again.

"You want to come quietly, Princess Aurelia." The beady-eyed elder glared at me.

"And why is that?" I asked with disdain.

"You care for that criminal's wellbeing, do you not?" he asked so casually my stomach dropped.

Asher was still here? I thought Fenrick got him out. That was how they planned to keep me in line while they experimented on me.

Shit. I'm so fucked.

"Where is he?" I asked angrily but let them lead me from the cell.

I wasn't doing this for myself. There would be no hope for me unless I was somehow able to escape the elders. I did it for Asher. This was all my fault. He never should have been dragged into this. He'd been kind to me and look what it got him.

Bad things followed me around like a plague. People that showed me any form of kindness suffered for it.

Was Grey suffering? Did I care?

I couldn't deny that I did care. No matter how hard I tried to put him out of my mind and to think of him as my enemy, I couldn't.

The mark on my neck tingled as I was led out of the dungeon and to a room with sterile white walls and a bed in the center.

There were straps at the head and foot of the bed. Those were supposed to hold me down? Not likely.

A metal table stood to one side with instruments lining the tray. They looked like torture devices.

I struggled against the arms holding me tight. I was not going to let them strap me down and torture me if I could help it.

"Your friend will suffer." The elder strolled to the little table.

Fuck. What was I going to do? I didn't want Asher to be hurt but they were about to fucking dissect me or something.

I straightened my spine and moved to the bed. I sat down heavily with a sigh.

The men circled me and strapped me to the bed. The leather cuffs had some kind of enchantment on them because no matter how hard I tried, I couldn't break free.

"Magic is tied to your emotions. In order to bring it forward, we will need to invoke emotions," the elder said.

He picked up a scalpel, turning it over in his hand. A gleeful smile crossed his sadistic face.

He ran the dull side of the blade down my neck.

Sweat broke out on my forehead and I clenched my hands into tight fist. My stomach flipped as he continued to torment me with the blade.

I held very still and glared at him with defiance.

"You are just going to cut me and bleed me to see if this shadow magic comes out?" I asked.

It was stupid. I still had the damn iron cuffs on. How did he expect me to access my power with the iron draining me?

"I'll do whatever is necessary to get this magic out." He sneered.

"And how do you plan on getting my magic out with iron draining me?" I raised an eyebrow and pulled at my restraints.

"You imbeciles didn't remove the cuffs?" the elder roared.

The men around the room stiffened before springing into action removing the cuffs.

Relief flooded me instantly. The lack of iron touching my skin nearly made me groan.

Magic tingled in my veins and came easily to my fingertips in a crackling heat but didn't affect the leather straps still wrapped securely around my wrists.

"Easy there, Aurelia. You don't want to cause your friend more distress." The elder shook his head.

I took a deep breath and called my magic back to me.

"You want me to let my magic out and then threaten me when I do what you want? That makes a ton of sense," I scoffed.

He turned the knife so the sharp end was against my throat, and I gulped.

Pain blossomed when he nicked my throat, and a small trickle of blood made its way down my neck to pool beneath my head.

My magic flared to life but there wasn't anything new. It felt exactly the same as always. What was shadow magic supposed to feel like?

Would it be different?

It crackled against my palms as the elder studied me like a lab rat.

"Your healing works much faster when your magic flares. There isn't even the tiniest of scars there," he said in awe.

I stared at the ceiling, not even bothering to acknowledge his words. It was good information and I filed it away for later, but I refused to let him see my curiosity.

He huffed an aggravated breath and turned back to the metal table. When he turned back, he had a small hammer in his hand.

I thrashed on the bed, my hands lit with magic again. I wasn't about to let him smash my bones.

"Let me fucking go!" I screamed.

I pulled at the straps on my wrists in an attempt to get free.

"Hold her arms down with her palms down!" the elder barked.

I kicked out at one of the men moving toward me but the strap on my ankle didn't allow enough movement enough to actually stop him.

Strong hands banded around my arms, squeezing hard and I nearly cried out. I held it in, not willing to give the bastards the satisfaction of knowing that they were hurting me.

They saw me as a threat or a piece of property. I wasn't entirely sure which anymore, after the gleam in the elder's eyes when he talked about the possibility of shadow magic.

"You will be able to heal it." The elder grinned.

"Doesn't mean I want you smashing my fingers to see if any new magic will surface." I glared at him.

"You don't have a choice in the matter. You are at my mercy here, and your friend will suffer for any insolence you cause."

He was way too excited to have me at his mercy. What a sadistic asshole.

I kept my mouth shut and gritted my teeth, waiting for him to get on with it. I stared up at the white ceiling refusing to give him any further reaction.

"You're going to scream for me before all is said and done," he said conversationally.

He was enjoying the anticipation of the torture. He wanted my reactions more than anything.

I closed my eyes tightly and waited for the pain.

The elder chuckled just before my knuckles crunched beneath

the hammer and searing pain filled my hand, pulling a scream from my throat.

My magic flared to life and another scream met mine as electricity sizzled out of me and into the hammer.

A dam broke inside of me and magic unlike anything I had felt before bubbled out of me.

My back arched as the room was flooded with my power.

I opened my eyes just in time to see the hilt of a soldier's sword coming toward me. More pain flooded my head, and a loud crack filled the air.

Fuck, this fucking sucks.

CHAPTER 8
GREY

A shadow stood above me. "Did you think I wouldn't have taken precautions?"

I groaned as I sat up. What the fuck was Malcolm doing standing over me?

I blinked against the dim light and scanned the dank, dark room.

Where the fuck am I?

"What the fuck happened?" I shook my head to clear it.

"You and the protector were stupid and walked right into my trap." Malcolm chuckled.

"Where is Fenrick?" I ask scanning the room.

There was a small cot near a window with bars on it. The room was so small, I couldn't stretch out completely. It was maybe six feet wide.

"Don't worry about that, worry about yourself, shifter king. Tell me where Aurelia is hiding." Malcolm crossed his arms over his chest and glared down at me.

"You don't know?" I chuckled. "She's beyond your reach."

"No one is beyond my reach," he said smugly.

"You don't know?" I shook my head. I was going to enjoy taking the bastard down a peg.

I moved to cross my arms and metal clinked together. He thought he could chain me so I couldn't shift?

There weren't chains that could hold down the shifter king in this world or any other.

"I know more than you can possibly imagine, mongrel." He spat.

"Did you know that you have been banished?" I smirked.

He narrowed his eyes on mine. "What do you mean? That's impossible."

"Is it, really, though? You abducted the princess. Don't you think the king would retaliate?"

The king was a notoriously angry man and could hold a grudge better than anyone in Faery.

Did Malcolm think because he was the captain of the king's guard, he would be exempt from the king's ire?

He was stupider than he looked.

Malcolm's face turned red in anger, and he vanished from the room. Was he going to check for himself? He would be sorely disappointed that there was a troll guarding the portal and that he could no longer see it.

I stood and took two steps toward the door and the chains clanked against the floor. Taking another step, my ankle caught and pulled back.

My wolf growled inside my mind at the chains caging us, and I borrowed his strength and gripped the metal in both hands.

I pulled at the cuffs and at first, they didn't budge but after I twisted hard, the sound of scraping metal filled the quiet place as the metal broke off at my ankle.

Reaching for the chains that were attached to the manacles on my wrist, I pulled with all my strength until one snapped then I did the same with the other.

I needed to find Fenrick and get out of here before Malcolm came back on a rampage.

A voice cried out behind me, "Master is going to be very angry."

I spun to the sound and found a brownie standing with his little hands planted on his hips as he glared at me.

"And ask me if I care. Why do you even work for a psychopath like him? Brownies are good and kind and respond best to those who are the same." I shook my head.

"Master bought the house, and I was included in the sale." He shrugged but he frowned at my words all the same.

"So, we're in Malcolm's house. It didn't explode?" I asked warily.

I needed to get as much information out of the brownie as possible before Malcolm got back from the portal.

"No, it did explode. The master used his magic to fix it." The brownie waggled his finger at me. "You should not have been breaking and entering."

"I didn't break anything. The door was still blown off its hinges from before." I scoffed and turned away back to the door. "All I did was enter."

I gripped the door handle and turned it. The door clicked open.

"You can't go out there!" the brownie yelled, exasperated.

"Who's going to stop me?" I asked over my shoulder.

The brownie looked down and away, showing submission as my wolf was close to the surface. He was no match for the predator inside me and he knew it.

I stepped out of the room and glanced around. There was no sign of Fenrick in the long hall.

Fuck. Where was he hiding the Fae warrior? We needed to get the fuck out of there.

I crept down the hell to the next door and cracked it open, but there was nothing there other than an empty office.

Could that be where he hid the book?

I pushed the door open even further and a squeak from behind me had me glancing over my shoulder.

"You can't go into master's office!" the brownie cried.

"Watch me," I said, and stepped into the darkened room.

There was a single lamp on the dark wood desk and bookshelves lined the walls. A high-back office chair sat behind the desk but my eyes returned to the books on the shelves.

I didn't get a good look at the book during the mimic spell, so I was going in blind. I needed Fenrick. He might know what the book looked like.

I turned back to the door and stomped out of the office, determined to find Fenrick before Malcolm returned.

"Do you know where the Fae warrior is being kept?" I asked the brownie over my shoulder.

"I cannot say," he mumbled.

I growled. I spun around on the brownie and picked him up by the throat.

"My mate is in danger in Faery and the Fae warrior is the only one who can help me save her. You will tell me where the warrior is. *Now*." My wolf was right at the surface.

"Your mate?" he wheezed.

He coughed and clawed at my hand.

"Princess Aurelia is my mate. She is trapped and I need to save her, but I can't get there without the Fae. So. Where. Is. He?" I snarled.

I dropped the brownie and his coughing increased as he sucked deep breaths of air into his lungs. He picked one hand up off the ground and pointed at a room down the hall. I raced down the hallway and pushed open the door.

Fenrick was huddled on the floor, the skin on his arms flared

red because of the iron manacles on his wrists. They were eating away at his magic.

"Fenrick," I said softly, and he lifted his head.

His eyes were black and the pupils unfocused.

What the hell had happened to him?

"Can you move?" I asked.

Fenrick shook his head and held up his arm.

I gripped both sides of the manacle on his wrist and called on my wolf's strength to bend the metal. It screeched in protest before snapping free.

Fenrick sighed in relief and showed me his other wrist.

"How did you get out? The last I saw, you were knocked out from the blast," Fenrick said.

"I woke up with that asshole, Malcolm, standing over me. My wolf helped." I shrugged.

"Where is he now?" he asked as I continued destroying the cuffs.

The brownie muttered angrily to himself every time a lock broke. I ignored him. He was being dramatic.

I didn't give a fuck about his dramatics. I needed to get Fenrick to the office and get the fuck out of that house.

"C'mon, you good?" I asked as I wrapped his arm around my shoulder and lifted him.

"Yes, let's get out of here," Fenrick said.

"We need to check his office first," I grunt.

"You think he would leave the book in the office?" Fenrick asked, incredulous.

"He's arrogant enough to do it, but probably not. We have to check, though." I stormed from the room and back down the hall.

The brownie followed closely behind me. "You can't take anything from the master's office."

"Do you want me to tie you up and gag you, brownie?" I asked.

The brownie gasped and stomped his foot angrily.

I opened the door to the office and turned back to Fenrick. "Do you know what the book looks like?"

Fenrick moved into the room and strolled alongside the bookshelves. "It's gold and priceless. I doubt it will be easy to find."

"Okay, let's look around quickly. He could be back at any time." I ran a hand through my hair and positioned myself by the door.

I was of little help finding a book that I had never seen in person, but I could keep watch.

How long would the troll be able to keep him busy?

"How is your magic, Fenrick?" I asked.

I had no idea how long it took to recharge after iron sucked the magic out of a Fae. It could take hours.

How long was he locked up there? Malcolm was a sick fuck, torturing a fellow Fae that way.

He really was a wicked bastard.

"It's returning quickly," Fenrick said, still scanning the books on the shelf.

"He must have a safe or something." I turned to the brownie with a wicked grin.

"I will not help you steal from the master," the brownie growled.

He tried to dart out of the room, but I was faster and picked him up by the back of his shirt. "You don't have a choice."

The little shit screamed and thrashed.

I shook him, trying to shut him up. His scream pierced my ears and my wolf whined in my mind.

The little fucker had a set of lungs on him. "Shut up before I shut you up. Where is the safe?"

"It's hidden with magic," the brownie said smugly. "You will never find it."

Fenrick strolled over and crossed his arms over his chest. "If you show us where it is, I can find it."

"No!" the brownie screamed again.

"What should we do with him?" I asked with a wicked grin.

I snapped my teeth at him in warning.

The brownie gulped but kept his mouth shut.

"He's been brainwashed and he's harmless." Fenrick shrugged.

I spun back to the door as a crash sounded from down the hall. The brownie laughed. "Master, they are trying to steal from you!" the brownie screeched.

I shook the little bastard. He was about to lead Malcolm right to us. Malcolm was the only one in the house who could sift, and the little asshole was giving him exactly what he wanted.

Malcolm appeared in the door, and I threw the brownie onto the nearby chair.

"How the fuck did you get out of the chains?" Malcolm growled.

"You underestimate shifters." I smirked.

I crouched into a fighting stance and grinned. My wolf growled in my head, thrashing at the barrier in my chest. He wanted to rip Malcolm apart.

"Rabid beasts," Malcolm snarled.

"The only one rabid around here is you." I smirked. "Where did you get that cut on your forehead?"

Fenrick chuckled. "Did you find a nasty little surprise when you went to the portal?"

"Fucking trolls." He narrowed his eyes at me. "How did you know?"

"Who do you think stationed him there?" I asked. For an ancient Fae warrior, he wasn't very smart.

Malcolm roared a battle call and magic flew out from him. Fenrick dove and smashed into me.

I flew back and hit the wall with a thud as flames poured from Malcolm's hands.

The man didn't care about destroying his house when he could just fix it all with magic.

Pain erupted up my spine and the breath whooshed out of me. Fenrick stood in front of me with magic of his own lighting his palms.

"Malcolm, you don't want to do this," Fenrick said, widening his stance.

"And why would you say that?" Malcolm sneered.

"Don't." I gasped.

If he told him about the book and what it held, there would be no way we could retrieve it and rescue my mate from the Fae.

"Aurelia is in trouble. She's gone," Fenrick said.

Fuck. The stupid Fae didn't listen.

"Fenrick, no," I groaned.

"She's in Faery." Malcolm shrugged. "It's inconvenient but not impossible."

What did he know that I didn't? Had he seen the book already and knew what needed to be done?

Shit.

"It's more than inconvenient. When did you become the Council's puppet?" Fenrick asked.

"I am no one's puppet. This is what's best for Faery!" Malcolm yelled.

He smirked a second later and waved a hand at the only exit. A wall of fire erupted, the heat searing my skin.

"Have fun burning alive." He sifted away.

What the fuck are we going to do now?

CHAPTER 9
AURELIA

My head pounded behind my eyes as I blinked them open. I ran a hand through my hair, but it got stuck on the caked-on blood.

As I sat up in my cell, dizziness nearly made me fall back on the cold stone.

Fuck. I was lying on the disgusting floor, cradling one hand with the other before realizing there was no pain.

Had my magic healed me?

I wiggled my fingers, and they didn't seem as if anything horrible had happened at all.

"You're awake," a gruff voice said from the other side of the wall.

"Who are you? I thought I was alone in here," I croaked.

"No, I have been here a very long time," the man said. "How is your head?"

"I'm a bit dizzy. What happened?" I asked, shaking my head and immediately regretting the action.

"I don't know exactly what you did, but they brought you in

here gushing blood from your head, unconscious." He sighed. "From the talk though, that elder got the shock of his life."

I touched my head and winced, the memory of the soldier's sword smashing into my head making me shudder.

"I lost control of my magic." I leaned my head back against the wall.

"I guessed as much. The way your fingers looked, I can't blame you," he replied.

I flexed my fingers again. "Who are you?"

"Just a fellow prisoner. I've been gone so long, I doubt you have ever heard of me."

"Why are you here?" I asked, because I may as well find something to do between torture sessions.

"I am apparently a danger to society as well as the elders' plans." He chuckled.

"Fucking elders," I growled.

I hated the old bastards and wanted nothing more than to destroy every single one of them.

I screamed as shadows slithered up my arms. What the hell?

"What? What's happening?" The man's panicked voice pierced through my screams.

"There's something wrong with my magic!" I cried.

I flung my hand, and shadows wrapped around the bars on the door. The bars bent under the onslaught.

"Breathe with me, Princess." A calm voice that was familiar but somehow different soothed me.

I matched my breath to his, doing my best to keep Grey's face out of my mind while I did exactly the same thing he always told me to do.

I slowed my breathing and the shadows untangled from the bars.

Shit, that is going to be noticeable.

Shadows slithered along my arms, pulsing against my skin. They were foreign but also a part of me.

"Are you okay, Princess Aurelia?" the man asked.

"I have shadow magic," I whispered.

"Shhh, Princess. You need to control it. They cannot see it." The man sounded panicked.

"They were trying to see if I had it. Why is it so important?" I asked him.

"I'll tell you, but you have to control it. Make it obey you." Gnarled, tan hands grabbed at the bars on his cell and stretched them just enough that they looked like mine.

I closed my eyes and coaxed the magic back inside me, desperate for the magic to listen to me. It couldn't be seen. I didn't know why exactly, but the man in the other cell was panicked about it.

Whatever was going on couldn't be good. The shadows slithered a bit more before seeping back into my skin.

"Okay, it's gone." I blew out a breath.

"Good. You mustn't let the elders see it, no matter what," the man said, sounding relieved.

"What is your name? How do I know I can trust you?" I asked.

"You should trust none but your mate."

I scoffed. The memory of Grey and his betrayal was still sending a knife of pain through my heart.

"I don't have a mate." I shook my head and slid down the wall, leaning my head back against it.

"You forget that I saw them bring you in. What do you think that mark on your neck means?" he asked angrily.

I must have hit a nerve. I wasn't sure that I cared.

"I know what it means, but trusting my mate is a bit tough right now since he betrayed me." I shook my head even though he couldn't see me.

"Impossible. Betraying a mate would be like chewing your arm off."

"Are you a shifter?" I gasped.

I thought all the shifters were sent to the human world. How was this man in a cell next to me?

"Yes. I was too powerful to exile, according to the assholes," he said with a growl.

He's been here since the exile? How has he not gone completely insane?

"Holy shit," I whispered.

"That's putting it mildly." He chuckled.

"You've been here all this time?" I was horrified.

I knew they were cruel, but that was going too far. What about his wolf? That would drive him mad.

"That's not what you really want to know, is it?"

"What's the big deal about the shadows?" I asked, getting straight to the point. "The court is the shadow court."

"It's been centuries since anyone has developed shadow magic."

There was a shuffling noise like he was moving close to the bars again.

"If they're the shadow court, how can they not have shadow magic? It doesn't make sense." I curled my knees up beneath my chin and wrapped my arms around them.

"They believe they have been cursed because they didn't stop the elders from exiling everyone," he said.

"If they think they are cursed, then why do I have the shadows?" I squeezed my eyes closed.

"The prophecy says the one who rules the shadows will decide." He sounded nonchalant.

"Decide what?" I frowned.

Was I supposed to decide who could live in Faery? That really didn't make any sense. I didn't know anything about this place.

"I think you already know, Princess Aurelia," he said.

I flinched. "Not fair. You know who I am, but I have no idea who you are."

"My name is Nickolas. The former shifter king," he said.

My jaw dropped open and I stared at the bars in shock.

The shifter king?

"What?" I cried.

Was that why the Council had locked him up for centuries? Why not let the former king go with the others? Why did they keep him here?

"That's why I am stuck here. Too powerful. My son won't come into his full power until my death, so they are keeping me here and alive until they can close the portal forever," Nickolas said with a growl.

"That's terrible."

How could anyone keep another person in a cage for so long? It was barbaric and cruel.

"It's okay, though. I'm here to meet you and help you escape." He had a smile in his voice.

"You're going to help me escape?" I asked, doubt creeping in my tone.

"Don't sound so incredulous. I don't know what my son did to betray you, but when we get out of here, I'll make sure to slap him upside his idiot head," he said, humor in his voice.

"Grey? Grey is your son?" I asked in horror.

He had to be talking about Grey. He was the only one I ever let get close enough to hurt me and he would be the last. I wasn't ever going to trust someone the same way I'd trusted him.

"Is that what he's going by in the mortal world? Yes, I can smell his mark on you."

Okay, that isn't weird at all. He can smell him on me?

I shuddered, not liking that at all.

"What the fuck? You can do what now?" I asked. "Wait, can everyone smell that?"

"No, Princess Aurelia. I'm stronger. And he's my son."

"That really doesn't make me feel any better." I squeezed my knees to my chest.

"Why don't you tell me what he did? I know my son, and he would never betray his mate unless there was no other option," Nickolas said.

"He was looking for a Fae to help him find something and sent a man to locate me. The man shot me with a tranquillizer dart and is the reason why the witch who raised me is dead and I had nowhere else to go." I shrugged.

If I tried really hard, I could probably find a way to blame him for this too. If I hadn't been running from him, I never would have been pulled into the portal.

The truth was that I was finding it difficult to stay angry at him. I missed him horribly. I tried desperately not to miss him, but it didn't help. My mark tingled at my neck, and I nearly groaned.

Where was he? Was he looking for me? I had already been gone much longer than I should have been.

"It must have been difficult for him to decide what to do. Who to choose between his fated mate and his people that depend on him to get them home," Nickolas said so softly I almost didn't hear him.

"Yeah," I said, but frowned.

Is that what happened? Did he only do what he did to save his people? Did it not matter that I was hurt in the process? Did it not matter that I was accused of murder because of his initial actions?

The lock on the door clicked. I widened my eyes and scrambled to my feet.

Shit. I'm not ready to go back to the torture chamber.

A woman in a dress that was practically rags walked in with her head down and chains connected to her wrists and ankles.

She had two plates in her hands and pushed them beneath the bars. I opened my mouth to say something, but the woman's eyes met mine and she shook her head imperceptibly.

Got it. Do not talk to the help. It could be bad for us all.

A buzzing caught my attention, and I cocked my head to the side.

It can't be, right? That would be too good to be true.

The woman left the room and I peeked at the food left behind.

Is it safe to eat or would they drug me? I can't use magic without something to sustain it though. Fuck, I'm so hungry.

"It's okay to eat," Nickolas said. "I don't smell anything foreign in there. Your friend is back, though."

"Friend?" I asked as the buzzing started again and a tiny blur darted forward, and all the air rushed out of my lungs.

Fiona glowed green and flew up to stare at me. "Oh, Miss Aurelia, you look much better than the last time I saw you." She blew out a breath.

"You've been here before?" I asked.

"She has," Nickolas grunted.

"Do not speak to the princess, disgraced king," Fiona spat.

I widened my eyes. That was another round of questions that needed to be asked. "Fiona, focus. King Nickolas has been helpful, but I need information. Have you seen Asher, and where is Grey?"

"Asher is back home but it doesn't look good, Miss Aurelia. Master Grey is gone. No one has seen him since we rescued Asher." Fiona fluttered up to my face.

Asher wasn't okay and Grey was gone? What the hell were we going to do without them?

Did I even want to live in a world where Grey didn't exist?

CHAPTER 10
GREY

Fuck. It's damn hot.

Smoke billowed up from the heat of the magical fire, choking me.

I could barely see my nose in front of my face as I coughed and hacked. Haze clouded my eyes, and I held my breath.

My wolf thrashed inside my chest as I crawled across the room searching for Fenrick.

"Fenrick!" I coughed.

Where the fuck did he go? He should be here.

"Grey, I'm here!" Fenrick called, but it ended in a hacking fit.

"We need out," I croaked.

This was complete bullshit. How was Fenrick not able to counter the magical fire?

Fenrick appeared in front of me, crawling on his belly toward me. "We need to go that way." He nodded to the door that was still a wall of fire.

"How the fuck are we going to get out of there?" I asked.

"I have a plan, don't worry." He turned around and crawled toward the wall of fire.

Should I follow him? How the hell is he going to get us past that?

I didn't comment again as I followed behind the Fae. Could I really trust him? Why was he helping me with my mate?

Could he really want everyone to return to Faery? Why?

It didn't make any sense. Why were the shadow Fae so willing to let us come back? Was it the shadow Fae as a whole, or just Fenrick going rogue?

He said that the king and queen sent him to retrieve the book and help my mate, but then why would they let the Council take her? Did they have a choice?

I came up behind him, keeping low to the ground. The smoke choked me as I waited for Fenrick to do something.

He got up on his knees and opened his palms straight up. Water gushed from his hands and hit the wall of fire with a hiss. We weren't out of the woods yet, though. The flames had spread through the hallway.

How long can Fenrick keep up the magic?

"I'm going to shift. Get on my back. I'm faster in wolf form," I said.

Fenrick tilted his head to the side in curiosity. It wasn't every day that a shifter allowed someone to ride on his back to safety. It showed immense trust.

I didn't trust the Fae, but we were both going to die here if we didn't do something.

"Okay, thank you, Sh- Grey," Fenrick said.

I was just glad he was trying to stop with the shifter king nonsense. I would deal with that title when I got my people back to Faery.

Quickly shifting, I bent my big body so Fenrick could climb on. My wolf growled, not liking the idea of the Fae on his back but didn't react otherwise.

As soon as Fenrick was securely mounted, I took off down the hall to the front of the house. A tiny, wailing voice hit my ears and I cursed in my head.

The damn brownie. That bastard Malcolm just left his loyal little servant behind.

"Grey, what are you doing?" Fenrick asked as I slowed.

He was still spraying water with his hands at everything in our path. I tilted my head to the side, where the damn little brownie was cowering in a corner.

"Shit," Fenrick whispered.

I trotted over to the little bastard and picked him up by the back of his tiny coat between my teeth and ran to the front door.

"Let me go!" The brownie squirmed.

"He's saving your pathetic life, brownie. I would be grateful and stop wiggling before he drops you in the flames!" Fenrick yelled, and the brownie stilled.

Fenrick hopped off my back and sprayed water at the front door as I searched for the tile that I stepped on before to be careful not to get thrown into an explosion again.

That sonofabitch Malcolm was sadistic and had zero regard for his house or anyone's life, including his misguided, loyal servant.

The man made me sick.

Fenrick opened the front door, and we sprinted out of Malcolm's house of horrors. I nodded for Fenrick to get back on.

"The car should be out here." Fenrick grimaced.

I knew that the car would be gone after Malcolm caught us. He wouldn't leave anything behind that would aid in an escape.

We would have to walk to the facility. It was the closest, and my penthouse was in the city. I wasn't walking through the city without clothes, so I wouldn't be shifting until we arrived at the facility.

Fenrick frowned but hopped back on my back. We never actually went to the facility, so he couldn't sift us there.

I tightened my jaw around the little brownie's shirt. My wolf would just as soon eat the little fucker than let him ride on my back.

The brownie whimpered, probably thinking he was going to be wolf food.

"Thank you for saving me, but I'm safe now and would like for you to let me go," the brownie said.

"You're coming with us, rodent. You have information we need," Fenrick said.

Good. Glad we're on the same page.

I ran through the forest with a speed and stamina of which only my wolf was capable. He raced between the trees, and I noticed there was magic in them that should not have belonged.

The trees passed in a blur until the magic of the wards washed over me and I slowed my pace.

The brownie was still screaming and cursing us, and my wolf shook him slightly. The wolf was enjoying terrifying the tiny annoyance.

Zeke met us at the front of the facility, his face drawn and his eyes tired.

He threw clothes at my feet. I waited for Fenrick to jump from my back and secure the brownie before shifting to human and dressing quickly.

A few of my shifters raced from the garage, and I nodded toward the brownie. "He has information we need. Lock him in a cell until I can question him."

The shifters reached for him.

Fenrick turned to me. "Do you have a magic-canceling cell? He'll be able to get out of anywhere else."

"You heard him!" I barked at the shifters.

The brownie flailed and screamed as they carried him off to the magical cells.

"Where have you been? We thought you were going to the

penthouse, but Freya and Fiona have been worried sick." Zeke crossed his arms over his chest.

"Fiona's here?" I asked, hopeful.

"She was but she went back yesterday when no one could find you." Zeke shook his head.

Fenrick raised a brow. "What do you mean, yesterday? How long were we gone?"

"You've been missing for two days," Zeke said.

"Two days?" I asked, shocked. "Shit."

"Where have you been?" Zeke asked.

"Malcolm got us. It's a long story. What did Fiona report?" I stomped into the parking garage.

Zeke and Fenrick followed closely behind me. How the hell had I lost two days in that house? I was passed out... but for days? What the hell?

Zeke sighed. "It isn't good."

"Just spit it out," I growled.

"The shadow Fae have lost access to their shadows since the exile," Zeke informed.

I turned sharply to Fenrick, who nodded.

"We have been cursed to lose the shadow magic we were created with. The gods were not kind to us after the exile." Fenrick rubbed a hand over his neck.

"What does this have to do with Aurelia?" I asked.

I had a feeling I really wasn't going to like the answer.

"They think she may be the one to bring the magic back to the court, and if she does prove to have it, the Council will kill her," Fenrick said softly.

"They want the shadow Fae to be weak. They don't want them to get their shadows back and they will do anything to keep them down." Zeke clenched a hand in a fist.

"What aren't you telling me?" I growled.

If I found out they were hurting my mate, I would tear the

fabric of the universe apart to get to her and destroy the elders.

"You don't want to know, Grey. I'm one of your oldest friends and I know that look. You need to calm the fuck down and think logically, or I'm not going to tell you." Zeke planted his feet wide.

We were stopped in the middle of the parking garage, glaring at each other. He needed to tell me what those fucks were doing to my mate before my wolf freaked out and forced a shift.

"I'm not telling you anything until you calm down." Zeke stared me down.

My shoulders slumped and I rubbed a hand down my face.

"Fine. Let's get up to my office and you can tell me over a fucking drink." I shook my head.

I stomped to the elevator and pushed the button. It wasn't coming quickly enough, and I stabbed at it again.

"Easy. That is not you calming the fuck down." Zeke clapped me on the back.

"I told you after the last few weeks, I need a fucking drink," I growled as the elevator dinged and I stomped inside.

I pushed the button for the top floor and leaned back against the glass wall then turned to Zeke with a grimace.

"How's Ash?" I asked.

I felt like a shitty friend for not asking sooner, but I just had a ton of information dumped on me.

"His body is still broken and he's in a coma. It doesn't look good." Zeke sighed.

"He will be back to his obnoxious self in no time." I grinned at Zeke.

He was a rider of the hunt, and those bastards were damn near impossible to kill. He wouldn't be taken down by the damn elders and their pathetic bullshit.

The elevator doors opened, and we stepped out into the empty hall. I led the way to my office and opened the door.

It looked exactly the way I'd left it, but it somehow felt empty.

But it wasn't the office that was empty, it was me. I was empty without my mate.

Would she even forgive me when we rescued her? I don't see how she could. I truly had done all the things she'd said.

I should have been honest with her instead of hiding my part in her foster mother's death.

Shaking my head to clear it, I grabbed a bottle of scotch and three glasses from the drawer in my desk. I poured the glasses and handed them out to the others. I took a sip and then glared pointedly at Zeke.

"Okay, I'm calm. What did Fiona report?" My hand tightened on the tumbler as I waited for him to speak.

"Aurelia doesn't have her full magic as she is yet to turn twenty-five. They are trying to pull it out of her." Zeke rubbed the back of his neck.

"Speak plainly, Zeke. I need to know what's happening to her." I sat forward, resting my elbows on the desk.

Zeke eyed Fenrick with distrust before he turned back to me with a frown.

"Fiona said they were torturing her. The last she saw Aurelia, she'd been beaten and left in her cell." He stood with his hands raised.

I vibrated with rage and the glass shattered in my hand, dark amber liquid pooling on my desk.

They were torturing my mate, and there wasn't a damn thing I could do to stop them.

"We need that fucking book because I'm going to tear every last one of those fuckers to shreds."

CHAPTER 11
Aurelia

I was numb. I sat in the cell with my back to the bars and stared into space.

"Aurelia," Fiona said, patting my cheek. "You need to stop."

I peered down at my hands with a frown. Shadows pooled there, writhing up my arms.

"Shit." I panicked, and Nickolas's sudden intake of breath made me pause.

Did he smell something?

Shit. Shit. Shit.

I did my best to call the shadows back inside me as keys jingled on the other side of the door.

"Fiona, hide," I whispered fiercely.

She buzzed up to the top of the bars, sat there and stopped the buzzing of her wings.

The same beady-eyed elder from before strutted like a damn peacock into the dungeon with three soldiers.

"Leave her," Nickolas growled. "She won't change until her birthday. You can't force the magic to manifest."

"Shut up, shifter king," the elder sneered.

He said the title like it was an insult and maybe it was to him.

"It's okay, Nickolas, I don't have a choice. He knows nothing will happen. He just wants to punish me." I shrugged and stood.

I stepped away from the bars as the elder jingled the keys, taunting me.

I kept my expression blank. I was starting to wonder if Malcolm was working for these psychos.

He had the same ideals as these idiots.

The door to the cell opened, and the men stormed inside, placing cuffs on my wrists before dragging me out of the cell.

"Don't do this, Ronaldo!" Nickolas yelled. "You have no idea what you are doing here."

His name is Ronaldo? That just fits him perfectly.

I almost smirked at the name but held my expression.

Nickolas continued to yell at the guards and the elder, but they ignored him.

I needed to focus. I couldn't let my shadows out during the torture session, no matter what. Even if he broke my hand with that damn hammer again, I couldn't let them see the shadows. It would spell the end for me.

They turned down a long hallway that I hadn't seen before, and I frowned.

This wasn't the way to the torture room. Where were they taking me? I struggled against the guards, who tightened their grip on me.

"Where are we going?" I asked, infusing as much haughty attitude into my tone as I could.

"You will be tried for bringing that criminal into Faery." Ronaldo sneered.

"You're going to charge me with a crime that I had no knowledge of?" I asked indignantly.

I hadn't even meant to bring Asher with me. I never meant to come here at all.

"You have broken our laws and must be punished accordingly." Ronaldo grinned maliciously.

"Where is Asher?" I asked. "Will he be at this hoax?"

"The criminal will not be there." Ronaldo waved a hand dismissively.

"You don't have him anymore," I said as realization struck.

They had fooled me into thinking he was there to guarantee my cooperation, but he wasn't there at all.

What happened to him? Did Fenrick get him back home?

I hoped so. Even if they decided to execute me, I was glad that he was where he belonged, hopefully in one piece.

"That is preposterous. No one escapes the Council. We have him to ensure your cooperation," he said.

"That's a lie." I grinned.

I didn't have to cooperate anymore and as soon as I got the opportunity, I was going to bust out of their cell.

My shadows had proven they could bend the bars.

Ronaldo stopped in front of an ornate door. Whispers trickled through from the room on the other side.

How many people were there to see this sham of a trial?

Without Fenrick and Asher, there they had no proof that brought him here when it was against the law. But I had no delusions that anything about this was going to be fair.

Ronaldo opened the door with a flourish, and gasps rang out in the room.

My parents were there, and they stood shouting angrily at the elders.

"You dare treat the princess of the shadow court with such disrespect?" my mother screamed.

"You mean to start a war by treating her as nothing but a common prisoner?" My father vibrated with rage and loathing.

Something dark flickered over his hand, and my eyes widened.

Did they get their shadow magic back when the elders tortured mine out? That did not bode well for me.

I shook my head at my parents and widened my eyes at my father's hand.

My mother caught my expression and glanced down at my father before covering his hand with hers.

To anyone else, it would have been a gesture of comfort or solidarity, but I knew the truth. She was hiding his magic, for me.

She knew the stakes and what would happen if they found out I had the shadow magic.

They may just kill me anyway, though.

"Enough!" Ronaldo roared. "The princess has broken a law that has allowed us to live in prosperity for centuries and she will be treated like the criminal she is."

Ronaldo shoved me into a chair facing the crowd and my father growled. My mother whispered something and his face paled as he glanced down at the hand that she held.

"My daughter will not be put to death for something that was not her fault." The king squared his shoulders and held his head high.

"The punishment will be as we see fit." Ronaldo grinned.

"You will release my daughter to me. She will not be treated so poorly. You want war with the shadow realm?" my father roared.

"You would wage war over a daughter who remembers nothing of you and has become associates with undesirables?" Ronaldo scoffed.

"I wasn't given much choice when your puppet took me to a realm I didn't know of and left me to fend for myself." I shook my head.

"Malcolm left you to fend for yourself?" an elder with greasy, dishwater hair asked with a frown. "You were just a child."

"The same child some of you wanted to kill because I was too dangerous." I scowled.

"We didn't do that, and we voted to simply watch you and not kill the threat to our way of life," the greasy-haired elder replied.

"The problem with all that is that you all thought you could decide my fate and you chose wrong for your precious way of life." I chuckled.

"How were we wrong?" Ronaldo growled.

"If I had actually grown up here, I may have seen things your way, but you let your fear rule you and now you've inadvertently caused all of this." I shrugged.

The elders glanced between each other with trepidation.

Old fools. They were all old fools. They did this to themselves.

"You aren't endearing yourself to us, Princess Aurelia." The greasy-haired elder who told me they should have killed me as a child narrowed his eyes on me.

"You're going to find me guilty whether I am guilty or not." I clanked the chains around my wrists as I held my hands up.

My parents' eyes widened, and they shook their heads. They didn't want me to antagonize the elders, but I was running out of fucks to give.

"You don't believe that we are capable of treating you fairly?" Sir greasy hair from before asked with a frown.

"*Are* you capable of treating me fairly? I mean not you specifically because of the way you have spoken to me so far, but do you think the others are capable of putting their prejudices aside and listening to the facts?" I asked with a raised brow.

The elder with the kindest expression scanned the other faces in the room and grimaced. "You are probably correct."

Ronaldo scoffed. "Richard, how dare you?"

"The child speaks the truth. You have all become corrupt with your power." Richard shook his head in disgust.

The rest of the elders screamed at Richard, and the courtroom devolved into chaos of accusations and people screaming. I sat back in my seat and scanned the pandemonium.

They'd done this to themselves. I turned to my parents and my mother grinned behind her hand. She winked at me, and my chest warmed with pride.

She was proud of what I had done. Turning the elders against each other had been easier than I thought.

Three other elders stood with Richard, spitting insults at the three elders who were rabid to get a piece of me.

What would happen if they were split down the middle when deciding my guilt? Would I be executed or would they set me free?

I could only hope for the latter, but I wasn't optimistic.

"Enough!" Ronaldo roared. "Don't you see what she's doing here? She's trying to divide the Council."

I raised my brows at greasy hair. His face was turning an ugly shade of eggplant with his rage.

"Let's just get on with this farce," Richard, said waving his hand in the air.

"Farce?" one of the elders next to Ronaldo asked with a scoff. "She has broken our laws by bringing that criminal here."

My father stepped forward. "That is untrue. She was brought here at our order and had no idea what was happening when she was dragged through the portal."

Richard raised an eyebrow. "That doesn't sound like she knowingly brought a criminal here or that she even came here willingly."

"I didn't. I was running from Malcolm and stumbled on the portal, but I didn't intend to come through or bring anyone with me." I nodded at Richard.

"Can you really prosecute her for something outside her

control?" Richard asked, glancing between each of his fellow elders.

The men closest to him frowned and stared at me.

What were they thinking? Were they going to let me go? There were seven of them. Would it come down to one elder?

"Let's vote," Ronaldo said smugly.

What did he know that the rest of us didn't? Could he have one of the sympathizers in his pocket?

"I vote we release her to her parents." Richard grinned in my direction.

My parents gasped, probably not expecting that. I held my breath, waiting for a verdict.

They could still vote to kill me. Richard was just one vote.

Ronaldo's eyes bored into mine. "I vote execution."

That wasn't the slightest bit surprising. I raised an eyebrow at him, unconcerned as the others cast their votes.

Three voted to send me home and three voted for my execution. One man was left. He had a nasty gash on one side of his face, and he stood by Richard.

I held my breath as I waited for him to decide. I wasn't optimistic, but my fate rested in the hands of seven old men.

Conflict and guilt twisted his features as he cast his vote for my execution.

My mother screamed and my father hurled insults at the elder as the man who decided my fate hung his head in shame.

Scar man was in Ronaldo's pocket. He had to be. That was the only explanation for his outward sign of guilt.

Ronaldo grinned and called over the crowd, "The Council has decided the princess of the shadow Fae will be executed at dawn."

My father roared and my eyes widened as shadows crawled over his arms, writhing with menace.

Ronaldo gasped before glaring at me. "You are the girl of the prophecy, and for that you will die."

Ronaldo raised his hand and lightning sizzling in his palm. The other elders rushed my father to stop whatever he'd planned to do with his shadows.

I yanked at my wrists in a desperate attempt to free myself from the magic-canceling cuffs they placed on me.

Ronaldo roared and threw the lightning at me. I closed my eyes and prayed to the gods that this wasn't the day I died.

CHAPTER 12
GREY

"Where is it?" I growled at the brownie at my feet.

"You're just going to kill me either way," he whimpered.

I rubbed at my eyes in frustration. I'd been at it for hours, but the diminutive bastard refused to talk.

"I have no intention of killing you right after I rescued you from a blazing inferno," I said through gritted teeth.

Why wouldn't the little shit just talk?

I leaned back against the bars and stared at the ceiling. Maybe I should try a different tactic. I left the brownie's cell, locking it behind me when someone screamed my name. I turned and found Karma still sitting in her cell. She had a black eye and a bloody lip.

Had she been a problem for the guards? Is that why she was bruised and bloody?

"What do you want, Karma? You aren't getting out of that cell." I shook my head.

"I didn't do anything. I didn't know what that man had in store for us." Karma growled.

"You followed Layla blindly and for that, you stay in the cell. You knew what she was doing and still pretended to have no idea that Layla was behind her disappearance." I clenched a fist at my side.

"I didn't know that he was planning to make Aurelia trap us here," she argued.

"Did you know he beat her and locked her in a tiny room? I think your punishment fits the crime." I shook my head and turned my back on her.

The jaguar in her growled at the insult.

I strolled down the hall to the end and knocked on the locked and sealed door. Zeke opened it with a nod.

"Did you get anything out of him?" Zeke asked.

"No, he's not talking. He thinks I'm going to kill him." I sighed.

"That makes no sense. You don't kill people who are useful, you reward them." Zeke shook his head and closed the door behind me, sealing the prisoners inside.

Maybe he was right. Maybe I should show the little shit that I can be nice and then he would give me the information that I need.

"Have a good meal sent in there for him, and make sure Karma sees that he's being rewarded." I stormed down the hall.

"You're rewarding him for bad behavior while treating her like the enemy she is?" Zeke asked and chuckled.

"I'm showing her what disloyalty gets her while showing the evil little brownie exactly what he can expect if he cooperates," I called over my shoulder.

I stabbed at the elevator button and waited for the ding. I didn't have any information on the book, and they were torturing my mate in the Fae realm.

If she lost control as she had so many times before and she does have shadow magic, she's as good as dead.

The elevator opened and Dan stood on the other side.

"Good. I need to speak to you. You have a visitor." Dan glanced at Zeke.

Zeke was an intimidating guy to most, so Dan's reaction to him made sense. He stiffened as Zeke followed me into the elevator.

"I think this is a personal matter," Dan said softly.

"Zeke is here to help. He knows everything that we do about Aurelia," I said and pushed the button for the top floor.

"Magna is here, and she and Fenrick are waiting in your office." Dan crossed his arms over his chest.

"Good. I need to know what this prophecy is all about." I stared at the ceiling in the uncomfortable silence until the doors opened.

"I have some things I need to discuss with you on the business side as well." Dan held out a hand to hold the elevator door open when it opened.

"You know my top priority right now is getting to my mate. If you can't handle the job of second-in-command, I'll find someone who can." I waved him off.

"That's not necessary, boss. We do have jobs we need to assign though." Dan followed behind me.

"Get them assigned. There are employee files and job descriptions in your office. Research shouldn't be hard for you." I growled.

"Got it. I didn't realize I got an office as your assistant," he said, and I whipped around to face him.

"What exactly have you been doing, Dan?"

Was the facility falling apart while he was the second? How did he not even know he had an office?

"I've been getting to know the staff and looking for Malcolm. This place is crazy." Dan threw his hands up.

I opened the door to my office to find Fenrick and Magna whispering quietly, their heads close together.

"What's going on here?" I asked.

"You didn't tell me you had a half-Fae seer working with you." Fenrick glared.

"Seers aren't common here. It's a closely guarded secret," I said and moved to my desk. "Plus, she says cryptic shit more than she helps."

"That's unfair." Magna narrowed her eyes at me.

"Is it, though? You haven't told me the details of this prophecy, and my mate is in danger of being executed in the Fae realm." I raised my brow.

Magna gasped and her eyes widened. "She's in the Fae realm?"

"Yes." I turned an accusing stare on Fenrick.

"I was following orders from the king and queen. We had no idea that the Council would find out so quickly." Fenrick shook his head.

"Of course, they did. I'm sure there is an alert on the portal to let them know when the shadow princess came through. They've been planning this since the prophecy was spoken." Magna shook her head at the Fae.

"I need to know the exact wording of this prophecy." I ran a hand through my hair.

"I don't know the exact wording," Magna said.

"What about you?" I turned to Fenrick.

"I haven't been informed of the exact wording. The Council of Elders kept most of the information to themselves." Fenrick shook his head.

"Tell me what you do know," I growled.

"The shadow Fae thinks there is a curse on us. Ever since the exile, we have been slowly losing our shadow magic." Fenrick held out his hand.

Shadows crept over his skin and his eyes widened.

"What the fuck?" I asked, staring at his hands. "I thought you just said you didn't have shadows?"

Magna gasped. "They have brought the shadows out of her." Magna stepped away from me, her eyes were wide.

"What does that even mean?" I asked.

"She's the one who can bring us back to our realm, but only if the Council doesn't kill her first." Magna sat heavily in the chair and tilted her head back to stare at the ceiling.

"They are going to kill her," I breathed. "Hopefully, she knows better than to show them what she can do."

"There is a powerful ally with her," Magna said. "They will tell her what to do."

"Who's the ally?" I asked turning to her.

Who would defy the Council? Was she talking about Fiona?

"I can't see his face, but he is powerful. He will protect her as best as he can from a cell." Magna's eyes clouded.

I hated when that happened. She saw more than she would ever tell me, and it pissed me off.

"Have you found the book, yet?" Magna asked as her eyes cleared.

"No, the brownie isn't telling us anything." I ran a hand through my hair.

"It's in the facility," she mumbled.

I widened my eyes and turned to Zeke. "Did anyone search the little fucker?" I asked with a growl.

"I figured that would be the first thing your people would do." Zeke shook his head.

Fenrick raced out the door and down the hall with me hot on his trail.

Those idiots were going to end up in a cell next to Karma if the brownie had that book on him. How is it that he wasn't searched?

I stabbed at the button on the elevator contemplating just

taking the stairs but decided against shifting and running down ten stories.

It may have been faster, but I didn't want anyone to see me rushing through the stairwell.

The doors opened and I barely waited for the others to get in before I stabbed the button for the jail floor.

"We have been trying to get him to talk for hours and he had it on him the whole time," I said shaking my head.

"Let's just get down there and get the book from him." Zeke stabbed at the button.

He was as pissed as I was that my men hadn't thought to search the little idiot.

What if he had something on him that would help him escape a magic-canceling cell? He could have gotten out with the book.

I shifted restlessly in the elevator. If he got out with the book, we would have a problem.

When the elevator doors opened on the floor with the cells everything was quiet. I breathed a sigh of relief as I marched out into the hall.

I placed my hand on the scanner outside the door to the cells and rushed to his cell.

Karma started screaming at me about food and how unfair I was, but I narrowed my eyes at her to shut her up.

I opened the cell with the little brownie, who he sat there on his small bunk eating and stared up at me.

"What do you want now?" the little turd grumbled.

"You have been holding out on me, brownie. Where is the fucking book?" I took a menacing step into the cell and the brownie gulped.

"Your people took it from me." He glanced away.

"You're lying!" Zeke yelled. "If his people would have found something like that on you, they would have told him. Don't fucking lie."

Zeke grabbed the brownie by the back of his jacket and lifted him.

The agitated creature flailed. "Stop! You can't take anything from me."

"We can't? You are at my mercy, brownie. If you had told me where the book was, I would have let you go. You did this to yourself." I nodded to Zeke, who shook him.

"I told you!" the brownie wailed. "Your people took everything!"

That couldn't have been true. My people would have given me those things, right?

Zeke patted him down and frowned. "There's nothing here, Grey."

"Dan!" I barked. "Find the shifters who brought the brownie in and search their quarters. If I don't have that book in my possession within the hour, there will be hell to pay."

Dan ran from the cell to the sound of Karma's cackling. I tilted my head to the side and strode from the room.

I snatched the shifter by the neck and picked her up until her feet dangled from the ground.

"What do you know, Karma? Tell me now or you won't live to see another sunrise," I said with a growl.

"Not everyone here is happy about the Fae princess catching the boss' attention," she said between gasps.

I squeezed my hand tighter, cutting off her airway. I wouldn't be lenient with anyone who proved to be disloyal. I gave them everything and a way to prosper as long as they were loyal to me. This was how I was repaid?

Jealous females thought they could steal from me to try to get rid of my mate?

"Find the book and the shifters who stole it and bring them to me. I will take no more disloyalty. They will pay in fucking blood."

Chapter 13
Aurelia

When no shock came, I cracked an eye open. A wall of shadows stood in front of me, blocking Ronaldo from view.

Shouts rang out, hurting my oversensitive ears as my mother rushed to my side.

"Is that you?" I asked her.

"No, it's your father giving us a chance to escape." She reached a hand out to me and helped me from the chair.

Purple magic flared in her palms and the chains clicked. Tingles raced over my skin, and I breathed a sigh of relief as my magic flared back to life inside of me.

"We have to go to the cells. I need to get my friends," I said.

I turned to the door I'd been dragged through, dodging a fireball aimed straight for my head. The heat seared my skin as it came dangerously close.

"She's getting away!" Ronaldo roared.

I glanced at the elder over my shoulder as he threw more electricity at me. My magic flared and shadows wrapped around my torso, writhing in anger.

They shot away from me, meeting the lightning head on and it fizzled out instantly. That's why the elders wanted to get rid of shadow magic?

Or was it Ronaldo specifically? With no shadow magic in the realm, he was the most powerful Fae.

"Mother, do you know a way out through the cells?" I asked over my shoulder.

I had no idea how I was going to get out of there, I just knew I had to get to Fiona and Nickolas first.

"We will find a way even if we have to blow a hole in the wall, Aurelia." My mother kept pace beside me.

My gaze snapped to hers.

My mother is a badass. Good to know.

"Okay, but let's try a door first." I grinned, reaching for the knob that would lead us to the cells.

Pain exploded in my back and sent me flying face-first into the door. I cried out as agony exploded in my nose and the crunch of bone made my vision blur as blood, hot and sticky, gushed from my shattered nose.

"Aurelia!" my mother screamed and whirled on whoever was trying to kill me.

My magic pulsed within me angrily as I turned. Shadows writhed and dripped to the ground at my feet, pooling around me.

My nose had already begun to heal from my use of magic. I sucked in a breath as a twinge of pain hit me when my nose set itself back into alignment.

My shadows creeped across the floor toward Ronaldo as my father kept him busy trading magical attacks.

I wanted that motherfucker to pay for what he'd done to me, but we had a small window of time to get out of there.

"C'mon," I said, waving to my mother.

I reached for the doorknob again and pulled the door open.

"Aurelia, watch out!" my mother screamed and shoved me through the door.

I rolled through the hallway just ducking the rogue electricity that wanted to take me out.

"What about Father?" I asked as I stood and dusted myself off.

"Channing will be fine. If we want to get to your friends, we need to hurry." She grabbed my hand and pulled me down the hall the same way I came in.

I raced down the hall to the door to my prison and threw it open.

"Princess, what happened?" Nickolas stood abruptly in his cell.

"Nickolas?" my mother gasped. "How?"

"We don't have time for that," I said. "Fiona, come on."

Buzzing cut through the shocked silence as Fiona flitted to me. I wrapped my shadows around the bars to Nickolas' cell and let them do their thing.

"I'm guessing they found out about your magic," Nickolas raised a brow.

"Not my fault. You didn't tell me that every shadow Fae would get their magic back when I did. My father lost it a bit when they sentenced me to death." I shrugged, and my magic ripped the bars free.

An echoing boom filled the room.

"Fuck, time's up," I said and searched for an exit.

"We don't have time, darling." My mother fidgeted and pooled magic in her palms.

Nickolas stepped out of his cell and straightened to full height. He was even taller than Grey, which was a bit intimidating.

"Blow a hole in that wall," Nickolas said, pointing a finger at the far wall. "I'll watch the door to make sure we aren't ambushed."

The shifter king stepped past me and placed himself between me and the door.

"We all need to go." I clenched my fists at my sides and shuffled my feet nervously.

"We will, I'm just making sure you get out first," Nickolas said, never turning to face me.

What was he planning?

He better becoming with us, or I will be dragging his ass out.

I narrowed my eyes at him. I wasn't leaving without him. How would Grey react to knowing his father was still alive and in a dank cell?

"Katrina, blow the damn door open!" Nickolas shouted as more screams and blasts filled the air, becoming increasingly closer.

My mother took a deep breath and then hurled the magic at the spot Nickolas indicated. A deafening roar exploded through the prison as dirt and debris blasted me in the face.

I choked on dust and coughed as I waved a hand in front of my face.

My mother grabbed my arm and pulled me to the steaming rubble as Ronaldo and his goons appeared in the doorway.

"Go, Princess Aurelia, I'll hold them off." Nickolas waved me away.

I dug in my heels. No way was I letting them keep him a prisoner any longer.

Anger at the elders rushed through me hot and fierce as a tornado of my shadow and normal Fae powers spun around me, blowing my hair in my face.

"You will not keep him chained!" I bellowed, and magic shot from my hands, putting up a wall of shadow and elemental magic between them and Nickolas.

"Let's go," My mother pulled at my arm again.

She was able to get through my magic? Interesting.

Nickolas stared at the wall of shadows that the elders were trying to beat down with their own attacks for a millisecond longer before turning on his heel and racing toward us.

My mother stopped abruptly on the other side of the rubble, and I nearly ran into her. "What's wrong?" I asked.

As the dust cleared, my eyes widened. Ten of the elders' knights stood blocking our path.

How did they get there? What made them think we'd come out this way? Was it the explosion? There had been tons of them.

Nickolas stepped up next to me and removed his shirt.

"What are you doing?" I asked, shocked, and turned away.

"I'm shifting. I'm sure you know about that, being mated to my son." Nickolas chuckled.

"Mated?" my mother asked softly and shook her head.

"Now is not the time. We have ten Council guards waiting to haul me to my death," I said warily.

My new shadows slithered up my arms. The more I used them, the more natural it was to me. They caressed my arms and waited for instruction.

A wet nose nudged my hip and I turned. Nickolas' wolf stood almost to my chest. He was a russet brown color with grey eyes.

He snarled as one of the Fae warriors stepped forward, ready to pounce and defend us.

But, why? It couldn't just have been that I was his son's mate, could it?

Nickolas leapt in front of me, putting his huge body between the warriors and me. The men drew their blades and crouched at the ready.

I let the shadows and my elemental magic pool in my hands, twisting and writhing together like a dance.

I didn't want to hurt anyone. Well, that wasn't entirely true.

Given half the chance, I would have ended Ronaldo's miserable life.

Nickolas crouched low and snarled as my mother stiffened.

"Guards!" my mother screamed.

Three men appeared from nowhere in the armor of the shadow court and surrounded my mother and me.

We were still outnumbered almost two to one.

One of the Council warriors slashed out at Nickolas with his blade. Nickolas pounced, and chaos erupted all around me as the Council warriors attacked as one.

I threw a blast of shadows at one warrior, and they turned to chains that wrapped around his body, holding him tight.

I spun as the hair on the back of my neck prickled with unease then dodged the blade aimed to take my head off my shoulders and blasted the warrior with magic.

They didn't care about taking me alive. They would probably be rewarded by the Council for killing me in battle.

Not gonna happen, assholes.

Vines raced up the man's legs and he stumbled as they grew and held him to the spot. I spun around and bent my elbow before smashing it into the man's nose.

He fell in a heap against the vines, unconscious.

Grabbing the sword from him, I spun it in my grip. I wasn't great with swords, but I would have to make do.

I turned and scanned the area for my mother, who was battling with magic against another two guards. Nickolas stood, bloody, over a third, and her own warriors each were taking on warriors of their own.

A yelp full of pain and anguish filled the space and I spun to find the last Council warrior standing over Nickolas with a bloody sword.

I screamed and my magic burst out of me in an angry wave. There was no controlling it this time. It spiraled around the man, cutting off his airway and lifting him off the ground by his throat.

I couldn't stop it, and in that second, I didn't want to. I wanted the man's blood for what he did to Nickolas.

"Aurelia!" Someone shouted my name, but I barely heard it through the roaring in my ears.

Death. I wanted his death and nothing else mattered. Not even when my mother's face filled my vision.

"You got them, Aurelia. They won't hurt Nickolas again," she said soothingly.

I cocked my head to the side. The shadow knights all stared at me with wide-eyed horror in the midst of the sea of bodies.

I didn't do that, did I?

I shook my head to clear it.

"Aurelia," Nickolas whispered.

He was back in his human form, a bloody gash through his side.

"Breathe with me, Aurelia," he said.

It was just like Grey used to do, and I found I missed him even more in that moment.

I took a deep, cleansing breath and dropped the man held by my magic. I matched my breathing to Nickolas' until his started to stutter.

"What's wrong? Why aren't you healing?" I asked frantically.

My mother knelt next to me and laid a hand on my shoulder. "The Council guards' weapons are dipped in a poison that stops the healing process."

"What? No. He has to heal!" I screamed and placed my hands on his chest, but my magic was depleted. It stuttered out the moment I called on it.

"I'm sorry, Aurelia," my mother whispered.

"Can you heal him?" I asked hopefully.

Nickolas grabbed my hand and shook his head. "It's okay,

Princess. Can you promise me something?" He coughed and blood dribbled down his chin.

This was really happening? My only companion these last few weeks was going to die and there was nothing I could do about it.

Helplessness washed over me as tears pooled in my eyes. "What is it?"

"Take care of my boy," he breathed. "He deserves all the happiness in the world. Whatever he did, I'm sure it was out of duty to his people."

I nodded my head because words lodged in my throat, refusing to come out.

Nickolas smiled and closed his eyes.

A wracking sob violently tore out of me. How was I going to tell Grey that his father died protecting me?

It was so unfair.

CHAPTER 14
GREY

I paced the office, running a hand through my hair repeatedly.

"Did anyone find the fucking shifters yet?" I growled.

I glanced between the men posted in the office. Dan shook his head.

"They signed out half an hour ago saying they were going on a job." He stared down at his phone.

"Both of them? And no one thought it was suspicious? All jobs have been suspended because of Layla's death." I shook my head and continued to pace.

Zeke stepped into the room with a grim expression.

"Asher is awake," he said.

"That's good news. Why do you look like an angry toddler?" I asked.

"It's not good news. They told him things while they were beating the life out of him." Zeke folded his arms over his chest, glaring at something over my head.

Fenrick shifted uncomfortably in his seat. "What could they have told him that I didn't hear?"

"You're not going to like it, Grey." Zeke sighed.

"I don't like much of anything these days. Let's go see Ash," I said.

Turning to Dan, I added, "Check the shifters' rooms for the book and report back to me."

"You got it, boss." He nodded and left the office.

We left and made it to the elevator. I stabbed at the button and waited impatiently for its arrival.

"What did Ash say exactly?" I asked Zeke.

"I'll let you hear it from him. He was adamant that I not tell you first." The elevator doors opened, and Zeke walked inside.

I followed him in wondering what could have been so dire they he wouldn't let Zeke tell me.

Fenrick squeezed in just before the doors closed.

"I helped get him out of there. I think I should come too." Fenrick shrugged as he leaned against the far wall.

I pushed the button for the infirmary. "That's fine by me. I think he'll appreciate the company after being out for days."

The elevator doors opened, and Asher's loud laughter filled the entire floor.

"I guess we can say he's feeling better." I shook my head as I strolled to the door to his room.

One of the female healers was in there doing a scan, which was why he was in such a good mood.

"Ash, stop flirting with my staff." I chuckled.

"When the only thing to look at is your ugly mug, I have to flirt with every pretty girl I can." Asher winked.

The healer blushed a deep scarlet as she scurried from the room.

"Now you're embarrassing my staff." I rolled my eyes.

I made my way to the side of the bed and sat in the chair next to him.

Ash's face fell and his gaze darkened as some unnamed memory hit him. "Aurelia. The Council has her."

"I know. Fenrick told us when he dragged your heavy ass through the portal," I said, attempting to lighten the mood.

It wasn't just for Ash, but me too. Whatever he had to say, it was nothing good.

Asher turned to the Fae standing in the doorway and nodded to him. "Thanks for getting me out of there."

I raised both brows. Asher wasn't one to thank people for anything, but I guessed it had to do with the trauma he'd suffered at the hands of the elders.

"What did they do to you?" I asked, leaning forward on my elbows.

"This isn't about what they did to me." Asher sighed. "They have someone else locked up with the princess, Grey."

"Who?" I asked.

Why would I care who they locked up with Aurelia? I frowned in confusion.

"King Nickolas is alive," Asher said warily.

He ran a hand over his tired face.

"What do you mean? That's impossible. He was killed as a traitor to the light Fae crown." I stood and rubbed the back of my neck.

He'd vehemently opposed the removal of the shifters and witches and the Fae had killed him for being disloyal, hadn't they?

"He wasn't. The elders knew of the prophecy long before the information was leaked. They knew the shadow Fae would lose their magic but still forced acceptance." He stared at the wall.

"I don't understand how one thing connects to the other, Ash."

Fenrick stepped forward and cursed. "A new king can't come into power until the death of the old king. If he's still alive, the prophecy can't fully come to pass." Fenrick balled his hand into a fist, his expression murderous.

"You're telling me that my father has been stuck in a cell for centuries?" I asked with wide eyes.

"They kept him alive so you would never become king," Asher said sadly.

"And I'm stuck here with no way to get him or my mate out of chains?" I jumped to my feet with a roar and punched the wall so hard my hand crumpled it like paper.

Zeke stepped forward as if to stop me, and I shot him a glare. He raised his hands up in surrender. "I think we should all just calm down. We don't know anything for sure, just what they taunted Ash with."

"I need the fucking book. I need it now more than fucking ever!" I yelled.

Fenrick clapped a hand on my shoulder. "There may be a silver lining. Yes, you have been exiled, but the king has not. If you got his power somehow, you might not need the book."

"Yeah, if he dies. But the Fae are keeping him alive in a cell so he can't die," I said.

"That's a shitty thing to say, Fenrick." Asher shook his head.

They just got through saying he had to die for me to get his power, and I didn't really want it.

"From what I know of the prophecy, true royal mates would break the curse on the shadow Fae. I have shadow magic I never had before." Fenrick crossed his arms.

Asher blinked and frowned. "You have the shadows? They were taunting me, saying they were going to use my presence there to force her to cooperate."

"Cooperate while they tortured the magic out of her," I growled.

My wolf was close to the surface. He hated this talk of torture when it came to his mate. He wanted desperately to end any threat to Aurelia, but we were helpless to save her.

All was quiet until the elevator dinged, and thudding feet moved toward us from the hall. Dan peeked his head in, breathing heavily.

"We have a location on the shifters, but we need to hurry," Dan said between gasping breaths.

"How did you get a location?" I spun around and stomped to him.

"One of them left a scribbled note in their quarters." Dan shook his head.

"If I hadn't planned to kill them both, they would be fired for such carelessness." I thundered out of the room after Dan.

"They didn't leave the book behind, so they must have it on them. I'm hoping they aren't meeting to hand it off." Dan pushed the button for the elevator.

"If there is a note about where to meet, then I'm sure that's exactly what they are doing." I stepped into the elevator and turned.

Zeke and Fenrick followed close behind.

"Where are we going?" Zeke asked.

"Witchside, in the city. It's actually not far from where Aurelia lived with her foster mother." Dan leaned back against the wall.

"Why so public?" Zeke asked, shaking his head.

"To stop anyone from starting a fight and taking the book. That plan will not succeed," I said.

Fenrick turned to Dan. "Did the note say who they were meeting?"

The doors opened to the parking garage, and I strode over to my SUV. Four huge men wouldn't fit in one of my cars.

I grabbed the keys and hopped into the driver's seat, barely waiting for the others to get in before turning over the ignition.

"Put the address into the GPS and let's get the hell out of

here." I turned and pulled out of the parking spot.

The tires squealed as I drove faster than necessary to the main road.

The drive to the city was silent, and I was okay with that, was lost in my own head. We were this close to getting the book, but something didn't sit right about the note and the shifters taking the book back to Malcolm.

Did he even know the book was missing yet? If it wasn't Malcolm, then who were the shifters working with?

I pulled into the parking garage at my penthouse and decided we would walk from there. The address was close by, so it would be easier to sneak up on the exchange. It was nearly impossible to find parking in downtown Dallas anyway.

I turned the ignition off and stared down the men who came with me. "Dan, you and Fenrick go around the back and me and Zeke will go around the front. There should be no escape for them that way," I said and hopped out of the car.

The streets were bustling with activity as we strolled to the small coffee shop that was mentioned in the note.

They had an outdoor patio, and every seat was full, but the shifters weren't there.

"I don't see them," Zeke mumbled.

There was an alley along the side of the building, and I nodded my head toward it. Zeke caught my meaning, and we moved toward the mouth of the alley.

My shifter senses went wild. The scent of rotting food and garbage nearly made me sneeze, but the low voices were what had my attention.

The fact that they were in an alley in broad daylight where anyone could see them made me cringe. They were stupid and careless. I was glad they were as good as dead for selling us out.

"You promise we can go home for this?" one of the shifters whispered.

"I've already said that, mutt. Don't make me repeat myself."

I stiffened at the voice. I knew that sound but hadn't heard it in centuries. I turned to Zeke. His eyebrows were raised practically to his hairline.

He recognized the Council puppet's voice just like I did.

I stepped into the alley and cleared my throat.

"I see the Council fucks sent their best errand boy into my city." I held up a hand when the shifters moved to run. "You aren't getting out of here. Submit to me and I'll make your deaths painless."

The shifters gulped and glanced between each other before dropping to their knees.

"This is a private affair, shifter king. No one asked you," Erik said and stepped toward me.

"You shouldn't have come into my city and tried to turn my shifters against me." I shook my head as if admonishing a child.

"This doesn't concern you." He stepped forward.

"Doesn't it, though?" I asked with a smirk. "Your masters have my mate and sent you to get the only thing that could help me get her back."

The shifters tensed on the ground, still on their knees, as a searing pain exploded in my chest. My wolf howled in rage and agony.

I dropped to my knees with a savage roar, my wolf wanted to rip from my skin. The shifters in front of me howled a long mourning sound.

Fuck.

My father had been locked up for centuries, so how did he die? Anguish tore through me even as the power fueled me. It was too much power too quickly.

I screamed and locked eyes on the Council spy. They killed my father, and I would do anything, give anything, to make them pay.

CHAPTER 15
AURELIA

A bellow of rage filled the air as the Council descended on us.

I stared down at Nickolas, sadness and anger warring within me as Ronaldo cursed his dead warriors littered on the ground at my feet.

"The idiots killed the shifter king!" Ronaldo screeched.

He was completely unhinged about the death of the shifter king but not because he cared.

My father raced up from the side, his shadows coiled around him.

"Are you okay?" He glanced between my mother and me.

I shook my head, pain at what happened to Nickolas crippling me.

My father glanced down at Nickolas and gasped, turning sharply to Ronaldo.

"You have been holding him all this time?" my father roared.

"You don't get to question me, shadow king. I'm your elder," Ronaldo spat back.

His eyes landed on mine, and mania shone through his irises.

My father stepped between us, blocking Ronaldo from view.

"Move, shadow king. The Council has sentenced the girl to death, and now more than ever, she must die." Ronaldo raised his arms.

"Katrina, get her out of here," my father said softly.

"What are you going to do? You have to come with us!" I cried.

"I will, just a second after you. Now go." Father ordered.

My mother grabbed my arm and dizziness washed over me. The landscape spun away, and darkness clouded my vision.

What the hell was that? What did she do to me?

My head spun as I hit something soft and swayed.

"What?" I asked as I glanced at the vaulted ceiling above me.

"I'm sorry, dearest. I needed to get you out of there. I should've prepared you before I sifted us." My mother stroked my hair back from my face.

Oh, she sifted us. I should have figured that out.

"Where did you take me?" I asked.

I didn't think being back at the castle where they took me from was the best idea and if I was honest, I wanted to go home to the human world.

I needed to find Grey and tell him about his father.

Anguish ate at my gut and guilt for not being able to help him. If I hadn't used so much power when I lost control, then maybe I could have saved him.

"We are at a secret home of ours," Mother said softly. "It's safe, away from the Council."

"Safe from the Council? Is there even such a place?" I shook my head.

The Council would hunt me across realms to keep their way of life at status quo.

"It's as safe as we can make it." She sat next to me on the fluffy bed.

I nodded and sat up. I needed information if I was ever going to get the Council off my back. I needed to know exactly what was happening to me.

"Why does Ronaldo care so much about Nickolas' death? Nickolas said it was because of Grey but didn't get into details." I peered up at my mother.

"Long ago, at the height of the shifter king's reign, a prophecy was shared about his death. His death would bring about a new era. The elders don't like change and wanted to stop any new era that had anything to do with the shifters or witches," she said.

"Why did everyone seem so surprised that he was alive?" I asked.

It still didn't make sense. They kept him locked away instead of exiling him with the rest of the shifters and witches.

"Nickolas was to be executed before the exile. He was against the plan to get rid of the shifters and they charged him with treason. I thought I watched him die." Mother sniffled.

"They faked his death and pretended that the exile was the new era that the prophecy had spoken about," I said, putting everything together in my mind.

"I'm starting to think you're right on that."

"But that isn't the prophecy that's about me?" I asked.

"No, darling, it's different." She shook her head.

"Katrina! Aurelia!" My father's voice boomed from somewhere inside the house.

Mother jumped to her feet and ran to the closed door, throwing it open and calling down the hall, "Aurelia's room, Channing!"

"Are you sure that's wise?" I asked.

Magic pooled in my palms as I anxiously waited to see if it really was my father and if he was alone.

They could have been forcing him into giving up our location.

"Aurelia, are you okay?" my father asked from the doorway.

"Are you alone?" I questioned, craning my neck to peer behind him.

"Of course, you are perfectly safe, daughter." He shook his head and stepped forward into the room.

There was no one else in the hall behind him.

I blew out a breath of relief and released my hold on my magic. "I need to get back to the human world," I said softly.

Guilt ate at me. They had saved my life and all I could think about was getting back to Grey and figuring out a way for us all to be safe.

"Your mother didn't tell you?" My father smiled.

"Tell me what?" I frowned.

"The only place in the realms we would have a secret house away from the Council's prying eyes is in the human world." Father chuckled.

"What? We're in the human world? How? Where?" I jumped off the bed and raced to the window.

I threw the curtains open to beautiful green trees as far as the eye could see.

"We are in the Texas wilderness." Father came up beside me.

We were in Texas?

"Did you know where I was when you bought the place?" I asked softly.

If they had known where I was, why hadn't they come looking for me?

"What do you mean?" Mother asked.

"I grew up in Dallas, with a witch. It's in Texas," I said.

"You were that close this whole time?" Mother asked with tears pooling in her eyes.

"I was." I shook my head.

How did the witch mask my presence so easily? They were right here at times, and neither of us ever knew it.

"I need to get to the facility." I shuffled my feet anxiously.

"It's not safe." Father clapped me on the shoulder. "I'll go see if I can find the facility or your mate."

"It's warded, Father."

I couldn't let fear of the Council stop me from making things right with Grey. Despite the betrayal, I missed him, and I had a promise to keep to Nickolas.

Pain lanced in my chest at the thought of Nickolas. He had done everything he could to protect me, and it had cost him his life.

"You don't need to feel guilt over the king's death, daughter," Father said.

He squeezed my shoulder when I glanced up at him.

How did he know I was feeling guilt over that? It was true, but that wasn't the only thing I was feeling guilt over. If I hadn't run off, then maybe Grey's father would still be alive.

Would we have even known he was alive? There's no way to know any of that.

"Oh, what is that?" Mother asked as she plucked something from my shoulder.

Fiona buzzed angrily, held between my mother's fingers.

"Fiona," I gasped. "I forgot you were there."

"Miss Aurelia, I don't like being forgotten and tangled in your hair." Fiona glared at me as she struggled in my mother's hold.

"Mother, Fiona is my friend. Let her go please?" I asked softly.

My mother released her, and Fiona buzzed up to the top of one of the posts on the four-poster bed.

"Miss Aurelia, I can take King Channing to the penthouse. Maybe we can find Master Grey there," Fiona said in her tiny voice.

"That is a wonderful idea," Father beamed.

"What am I supposed to do? I don't want to just sit here and do nothing," I said, shaking my head.

"You could start with a shower," Fiona said in a disgusted tone.

"Hey, that's not my fault. I was in a fucking dungeon for weeks." I crossed my arms over my chest and scowled at Fiona.

"Doesn't mean you stink any less." She waved her tiny hand in front of her nose.

"Rude."

"I thought you said she was your friend," Mother whispered to me.

"She is. Things are a bit different in the human world, and friends come in unexpected packages." I chuckled.

"Very strange." Mother frowned at Fiona still sitting on top of the post, swinging her legs back and forth as her wings fluttered behind her.

"I want to know more about the prophecy that I'm involved in." I glanced between my parents.

They shared a look at my abrupt subject change.

"If I am going to stay behind while you go find Grey, I want to make good use of that time."

They weren't going to let me out in the world, but why? The Council never came to the human world, so I was safest there, right?

"Fine, let's go into the sitting room. I have a book in there that may help explain what I know for now." Mother looped her arm in mine and led me from the room.

"I'll bring your prince back, daughter," Father announced and then disappeared with Fiona on his shoulder.

Was Grey my prince? I didn't think he was technically a prince at all. Did he know that his father was dead? Did he feel the magic transfer? I hoped my father didn't explain to him what really happened. That Nickolas was dead because of me.

Would Grey hate me forever if I told him?

My mother nudged my shoulder. "Don't fret, darling. He will not blame you for his father's death if he is truly your mate."

"How do you guys do that? You know when I'm feeling guilty," I said curiously.

"The scent of guilt is acrid. It's very easy to discern." She shrugged and led me down a set of marble stairs.

"So, I smell? That's not weird at all. Maybe Fiona was right, and I should start with a shower." I shuddered.

"It's not a physical scent on your skin, rather more like our magic is empathic and the emotions come through in a scent. Not everyone describes it as a scent, though." She glided away from the stairs and into a small sitting room.

She stepped next to the black, overstuffed couch and sat gracefully on the edge of the seat.

Would I ever be that graceful and elegant? Probably not.

I fell back on the couch beside her and leaned my head back on the cushion. It was so nice to sit on something that wasn't stone or seriously uncomfortable. It had been so long I'd nearly forgotten what it felt like.

Mother grabbed a book from the side table and opened it in her lap. "I'm not sure if the prophecy about the king is connected to the prophecy about you, but it makes sense."

"What are you talking about?" I frowned.

"Think about it. The prophecy said the death of the king will usher in a new era. An era where you bring back the shifters and witches. Shadow magic comes back, and we live in prosperity." Mother shrugged, never looking up from her book.

Father appeared in front of us, a grim expression on his face. Fiona was crying softly.

"What happened?" I stood abruptly.

"The penthouse was ransacked, and Freya is..." Fiona trailed off and my heart broke for her.

"Freya is what, Fiona?" I asked, panicked.

"Freya is gone. I think someone took her," she sobbed.

"Was Grey there?" I asked, but it was a stupid question.

If Grey had been there, he would have come back with them.

Where is Grey and is he all right?

CHAPTER 16
GREY

"He's gone." I breathed through the pain.

"What?" Zeke asked with a frown as he leaned down to help me up.

My hands shifted to claws as I stared the Council spy down. "They killed my father."

I stood, barely holding my wolf back from shifting and tearing into the spy. He was beating at the inside of my chest, baying for the elders' blood.

Power unlike anything I'd ever felt before poured through my veins and I snarled.

"Shit," Zeke said. "He's dead? So it's happening then."

I took a threatening step forward. Erik glanced around the alley, scanning it for any possible exit. He wouldn't be fast enough to escape my claws.

"I was just sent to retrieve a book." Erik threw his hands up in surrender. "I didn't even know the king was still alive."

"No? Then why aren't you shocked by the power surge that just raged through me?" I sneered.

"I have no problem with you, shifter king. I just came to

retrieve the book." Erik took a step back but stopped when I growled.

"You two." I peered at the shifters on their knees. "Give me the fucking book. Zeke is going to detain you."

"Please, boss," one of them whimpered.

"You stole from me. You will be punished." I glared, holding out my hand for the book as the sound of running footsteps pounded the ground behind Erik.

Fenrick came into view first with a grimace. "Erik. Of course, they sent you."

"Fenrick. I see you are as much of a traitor to the Council as I always believed you were." Erik smirked.

"Detain the asshole." I turned back to the shifters.

They were going to pay for what they'd attempted. I stomped forward, picking the shifter on the right up by his throat.

"Tell me where the book is," I snarled.

He glanced to the other shifter almost reflexively, and I threw him on the ground at Zeke's feet.

The second shifter stiffened as I stomped to him.

"Zeke, detain him!" I called over my shoulder to the rider.

Reaching down, I ripped the bag off the shifter's shoulder.

Fenrick shouted, "Erik, you don't want to do that!"

I glanced up to see Erik with magic crackling over his palms.

"You want to challenge me?" I laughed.

I threw the bag to Zeke so he could check it for the book. If the shifter lied to me, his death would be even more painful. I would guarantee it.

"I need that book," Erik growled.

"You just watched me become the new shifter king. Do you really think you're fast enough to challenge me?" I shook my head.

Erik glanced away, unsure. Fenrick frowned in confusion at my words.

"He's dead?" Fenrick asked softly.

"Apparently, something happened. I need to get the book more than ever now because he was with my mate in those cells," I growled.

Was my mate dead too? Did she escape and my father helped her? I really hoped it was the latter.

Aurelia's death would be unacceptable. I would rage against both worlds if something had happened to her.

Zeke clapped me on the shoulder. "I have the book. Let's get them rounded up and get out of here."

"No!" Erik yelled, startling me.

I turned just in time to watch him throw crackling electricity right at Zeke. I shoved the rider hard out of the way then with speed I never possessed before, ran to Erik, gripped him by the throat and threw him against the brick wall.

His head cracked and his eyes rolled back in his head.

I turned to Zeke to make sure that he still had the bag in his hand. He had the bag in one hand and the other was wrapped around the shifter's neck.

Dan stepped forward, peering down at his phone.

"I received an alert from the security company that oversees the building you live in." Dan frowned.

"What's going on now?" I growled.

I nodded to Fenrick, who was standing over Erik, letting his magic wrap around the Council spy's unconscious form.

"Someone broke into your penthouse," Dan said.

"What the fuck?" I growled.

I was torn between checking on Freya and securing the book and the supernaturals who needed to be punished.

Fenrick glanced at me with a nod. "Go. We can handle things here."

"Are you sure?" I asked.

"Yes, now that I know where the facility is I can sift there."

Fenrick reached down and grabbed Erik, throwing him over his shoulder.

He sifted away, and I turned to the mouth of the alley. I needed to get to the penthouse. It was urgent that I make sure Freya was okay.

I rushed the two blocks to the building, trying not to run supernaturally fast. There was no way to explain that to the humans in the area.

We needed to keep the humans unaware of us. Gods only knew what would happen if they discovered our existence.

The elevator from the parking garage took too long. I ran a hand through my hair as I watched the numbers change with the passing of each floor.

I tapped my foot nervously.

Fuck. Is Freya okay?

The elevator finally dinged, and I raced into the entryway. My home was in complete disarray... again.

What the fuck? Who trashed my apartment?

"Freya?" I called into the room.

Furniture was overturned and slashed. Feathers and stuffing littered the room, but it was just furniture. It was replaceable.

Freya was what I was really concerned about. "Freya?"

I crossed to the kitchen where she would normally have been.

Where the fuck is she? Did she get taken again?

The kitchen was just as destroyed as the living room and entryway. Everything was torn from the cabinets.

Why would someone do that? It's not like I would hide things in the kitchen.

This wasn't simply a robbery. Someone wanted to send me a message. This was personal.

"Freya!" I yelled and ran to the hall just as Zeke, Fenrick, and Dan stepped out of the elevator.

"She's gone." I sighed.

Who would take the sprite from my home?

Fenrick cocked his head to the side. "Can you smell anything, shifter king?"

I growled because no, I didn't try to scent the intruder. I hadn't had the heightened senses long enough to really think about scenting the air for anything.

"I forgot my senses are even more enhanced now," I admitted.

I took a deep breath through my nose and growled at the scent.

"Malcolm," I rumbled.

"Of course, that rat bastard would come here." Zeke shook his head. His hands balled into fists at his sides.

"How did he know where you lived?" Fenrick frowned.

"This isn't the first time that fucker has broken into my home and taken someone important to me."

My hands turned to claws and I roared out my anger.

"He's after the book. I bet he plans to trade Freya for it." Dan shook his head.

"He's not getting it. Freya will be pissed if I give up the only thing that could bring us to Aurelia." I shuddered, wondering what pranks she would pull on me in the process.

It would not be pretty.

"That sprite gets angry pretty easily. I wouldn't want to be you if she was pissed at you." Dan grimaced.

"What are we going to do?" Fenrick asked. "We can't give him the book, but we can't let him keep your friend, either."

"I don't know, we could pretend we are giving him the book and get the sprite back by force." Zeke crossed his arms over his chest.

"That could be an option, but he's not stupid. He'll expect us to try to double-cross him." Fenrick ran a hand through his hair roughly.

"You don't become the captain of the king's guard by being stupid," I agreed.

Buzzing hit my oversensitive ears and my head snapped to the hall.

Was that Freya? Did Malcolm not have her after all?

"Freya?" I called, hope filled my tone. Did she somehow escape the madman?

A buzzing ball of green flew down the hall with a beaming smile. Fiona crashed into me, excited.

"We thought you were gone!" Fiona screeched.

"Fiona? What are you doing here?" I asked, confused. She was supposed to be in Faery, helping Aurelia.

"I can answer that," a male voice said, which made me stiffen.

I turned. How the hell was the king of the shadow court standing in my living room?

"Where is Aurelia?" I asked with wide eyes.

Her father was standing right in front of me. How was he here with me?

"She's safe. We have been looking for you," the king said.

Fenrick dropped to one knee, seeing the king, and I scowled at him.

"Where is she?" I asked angrily.

I was a king too now, so I didn't have to bow to the shadow king.

"She's at our safe house. She's fine. I will take you to her." The shadow king nodded to Fenrick, and he stood.

"My king, what has happened since I last saw the princess?" Fenrick asked softly.

"Much has happened, but we must leave before Malcolm returns." The king turned.

I eyed Zeke. "Can you keep track of the book, and you and Dan don't let anyone in the facility know where it is."

"You got it. What happens if Malcolm reaches out about Freya?" Zeke frowned.

"Try to trade for his brownie, though I doubt he cares about the servant who is so loyal to him. Stall as much as possible, and call me if there is a new development. I need to see my mate."

Zeke nodded and he and Dan walked into the open elevator.

"Okay, shadow king. Let's go. I need to see my mate," I said.

My wolf howled in my head, excited about seeing his mate and wanting to shift. I refused to let him out, even though he was stronger than he had ever been before.

Fenrick wrapped a hand around my arm and sifted. He obviously knew where the king's safe house was.

Dizziness washed over me as we landed in a cozy living room. Fiona lifted off my shoulder as we touched down, and I followed her progress to the couch.

My shoulders straightened and my eyes widened as I stared down at my mate sitting on the plush, overstuffed couch.

Her green eyes bored into mine and I stood rigid.

Is she still angry at me? I can't tell based on her expression. What is she thinking right now?

"Grey?" Aurelia whispered.

My wolf howled in my mind. He was frightened that she would be angry and not want anything to do with me.

"Aurelia," I breathed.

She gave nothing away as she stood slowly.

I clenched my fists at my sides so I didn't reach for her. She had every right to be angry with me and accuse me of betrayal.

She stepped in front of me slowly, not quite meeting my eyes.

"You're okay? Your father..." she trailed off, glancing away.

"I know, I felt the transfer of magic. What happened?" I asked, even though that wasn't what I wanted to know.

Her face fell and tears pooled in her eyes. I reached up a hand and cupped her cheek.

"He... he died trying to protect me," she whispered brokenly.

"I'm sorry, that must have been difficult for you," I said tentatively, pulling her close.

She let me tug her into the circle of my arms and I breathed a sigh of contentment.

She was finally back, and she wasn't pushing me away.

CHAPTER 17
AURELIA

Grey was here and holding me in his arms. He didn't get angry that his father had died to protect me, he just held me close.

How could he not be angry with me though? It was my fault his father was gone.

I pulled back and stared up into his eyes. So many emotions and questions passed between us in that moment.

Was I still angry with him? If I was honest with myself, I hadn't been angry for a while.

I sighed and laid my head back on his chest, listening to the thumping of his heart. Grey's arms tightened around me as a throat cleared.

"Sorry to break up the reunion, daughter, but we have things to discuss." My father clapped Grey on the shoulder.

"Right, sorry." My cheeks heated as I took a step back, but Grey refused to let me go.

Grey growled softly as I pulled away from him and sat on the couch beside to my mother. He sat down next to me, crowding me and intwining our fingers.

Did he think I was going to leave? I had no intention of ever leaving him again. Not only because of the promise I made to his father, but because I needed him. His betrayal didn't seem so great in the scheme of things. He did it for his people and didn't know how to tell me. I could forgive that.

"What do we need to discuss?" Grey asked, tightening his fingers around mine.

My father blew out a breath before turning to Grey.

"Aurelia is the princess from the prophecy and has brought back shadow magic to our people, but I fear we are going to have a war with the elders as they sentenced her to death."

"They sentenced her to death? For what?" Grey stiffened next to me.

The growl in his tone meant his wolf was close to the surface. I patted his hand to soothe him.

"For no other reason than I was a threat to their way of life. They trumped up charges of me bringing Asher with me into Faery," I said.

My eyes widened and I snapped my gaze to Grey. "Asher?"

"He's going to be fine. He's already being a pain in the ass." Grey shook his head with a small smile.

"We need to gather our forces," Father said.

"The syndicate is having some staffing issues at the moment." Grey grimaced.

"But you do have people trained for battle, yes?" my father asked with a raised brow.

I slumped back on the couch not wanting to go back to that place. Every time I went there something bad happened.

"Yes, but what good will that do us if we can't get through the portal?" Grey squeezed my hand.

He must have seen my reaction to the place. I hated the facility.

Fenrick ran a hand over his face. I almost forgot he was there he was so quiet.

"We have access to the book now. We could probably find a way to get everyone back in through the portal, but the Council watches it as closely as we did."

"You have the book? Where?" Father asked with wide eyes.

He turned, glancing between the two men.

"I wouldn't take it with me to my home that had been ransacked." Grey sat back, his shoulder brushing mine and sending tingles down my spine.

"Fair enough." Father nodded. "We need the book."

"What about Freya?" I asked softly.

"I have people on that already, but I have a feeling the only way we are getting her back is if we pretend to trade for the book." Grey sighed.

"I think we need to go to this facility and get the book." Father stood from his chair.

"Right now?" I glanced out the window at the darkening sky.

I wanted to put that off as long as possible. I hadn't even had a chance to talk to Grey yet.

"Daughter, we need to do this quickly. They will continue to send their men after you. They want you dead." Father crossed his arms over his chest.

"You're right. I know you are, but I just don't like that place," I said, glancing down at my hands in my lap.

Grey wrapped an arm around my shoulders and pulled me close. "We don't have to go now if you don't want to, but King Channing is right. We need to move quickly on this."

"No, it's fine. Let's go. I need to train anyway." I hadn't trained in weeks and still didn't know how to do things that other Fae could.

"That, you do." Father smiled at me.

He turned to Fenrick. "You have been there, yes?"

"Yes, my king. I will take you there first so you can help take them there." Fenrick bowed his head to my father.

He clapped a hand on my father's shoulder and sifted away. I stood and strolled to the window. What would happen when we got to the facility?

"You okay?" Grey asked, stepping up behind me.

"I'm fine." I sighed.

"Are you really? Are we good or..." He trailed off.

Is he afraid to ask that question?

I turned and leaned against him. "We're good. I should have let you explain. I was just in shock seeing the stalker in the facility after the horror show of Layla's death."

"You were so angry at Dan, and I didn't want you to leave. It really wasn't malicious." He wrapped his arms around me and rested his chin on my head.

My mother stood with a smile on her face. "You two will definitely bring in a new era for all of us."

"What?" Grey asked with a frown.

"Your father's death was foretold to usher in a new era for Faery." My mother patted his shoulder.

"One thing at a time, Mother," I said, shaking my head.

Father and Fenrick sifted back then, and I pulled away from Grey. I needed to learn to sift like they could. It would make things so much easier.

Fenrick clapped Grey on the shoulder and my father wrapped his arms around Mother and me.

The room spun out of focus quickly and I closed my eyes against the dizziness that always took hold when someone sifted me.

I stumbled as we appeared on the dirt road outside the wards of the facility. My father's arm tightened around me to steady me.

"Not quite used to that?" he asked with a grin.

"No, I never had anyone to teach me how to use my magic." I shrugged.

"I'm sorry for that," Father whispered.

Why was he sorry? It wasn't his fault that Malcolm abducted me and then left me in Dallas to fend for myself.

Grey stepped next to us. "We need to get inside the wards before Malcolm shows up and we have a fight on our hands."

"Malcolm will pay," my father growled.

We rushed to the other side of the wards even with that growled threat.

I breathed a happy sigh as the trees danced in the breeze bathed in moonlight. It was my favorite place.

This forest spoke to me in a way no other forest had, not that I had been in many forests. There was something magical about that place though.

Grey wrapped his hand around mine, probably more for my comfort. The previous time I had been here was not a fun experience.

The last person I expected to see rushed toward us with a huge grin on his face. The mountain of a man grabbed me away from Grey and spun me around.

"Shouldn't you be resting?" I asked Asher with a giggle, hugging him tightly.

"Zeke told me you escaped the Council and I've been waiting to see you." He grinned and set me back on my feet.

Grey growled and wrapped his arms around me possessively. "Don't do that again."

"We went through trauma together. I'm allowed a friendly hug." Asher crossed his arms over his broad chest.

I swatted at Grey's arms around me. "He's my friend and I was worried about him. Stop it."

Possessive wolf.

"Fine," Grey grumbled but didn't let me go. "Where is Zeke?"

"He's in your office." Asher nodded his head in the direction of the parking garage.

Asher glanced between all of us, and his eyes widened as they landed on my parents. His shoulders stiffened and he peered at me with a question.

"They helped me escape," I said.

"I'm just shocked to see them in the human world." Asher turned back to the parking garage.

We walked through the space, dread filling me as we stepped into the elevator.

Grey pushed the button for the top floor and pulled me into his side. It made me feel slightly better.

When the doors opened, Grey ushered me out first and we walked down the deserted hall.

I stopped short, stiffening when we walked into the office. The man who shot me with the tranquillizer dart was standing by the huge window.

"Shit," Grey whispered. "I forgot he was here."

I took a step back and scanned the room. What did I want to do? I wanted to run again. Panic tugged at my insides like claws.

"Princess," the man said and dropped to his knee.

"What the fuck?" I asked, turning to Grey with wide eyes.

"Dan is half Fae," Grey said. "He's bowing to royalty."

"Make him stop." My voice rose in pitch.

I took two large steps back. I needed to get out of there. My throat dried up and I gasped for breath. Shadows slithered up my arms angrily with my panic.

Grey turned me to face him. "Breathe with me."

His words were so soft, they helped calm some of the distress but also left a pang of sadness in my heart.

Nickolas had helped me the same way when I panicked. I glanced down but Grey pinched my chin gently, turning my face to meet his eyes.

"Keep your eyes on me and match my breathing." Grey breathed in deeply and blew it out slowly.

"You still need to make him stop," I said but did as he directed.

"I think it's his way of apologizing."

I nodded my understanding and continued to breathe with Grey. Slowly, the magic slithered away until it was completely gone.

Why did I panic so badly? I told Grey on more than one occasion that I wanted the man dead. Maybe I wasn't as strong and brave as I thought.

"I'm okay now," I said with a small smile.

"Are you sure?" he asked and kissed my forehead.

"I am." I turned to Dan, who was still on the ground, and grimaced. "You can get up now."

The man didn't get up right away and I turned back to Grey.

"Dan, get off the ground. You're making her uncomfortable." Grey shook his head.

He finally stood and I breathed a sigh of relief.

"I'm sorry for my part in your foster mother's death, Princess Aurelia. Truly." Dan bowed his head.

"This isn't what we came here for." I turned back to my father.

"What did this man do?" Father asked.

"I shot her with a tranquillizer dart," Dan said.

King Channing took a threatening step forward and reached for Dan. He was so quick, no one could stop him. He had Dan around the throat and lifted him off the ground.

"Father, stop!" I yelled, rushing to grab his arm.

"He shot you," my father growled.

"I know, but it's over now." I finally succeeded in getting him to lower him back to the ground, but he still had his hand cutting off Dan's airway.

"You're lucky she's so forgiving. In my court any slight on my family is punishable by death." The king pushed him away roughly.

Grey just stood there, arms crossed over his chest and a smirk on his face. Dan coughed and gasped, bent at the waist, trying to get air in his lungs.

"It's less than you deserve for that particular stunt." Grey shook his head.

I turned to him sharply. He was the one who sent Dan after me. How could he say such a thing?

"Grey," I said with a raised brow.

"I didn't order him to shoot you with a dart. I didn't even find out he'd done that until you told me." Grey moved to the desk and sat behind it, pulling me down with him.

Father raised a brow but didn't comment.

"We have more pressing things to deal with," I said.

Like starting a damn war with the elders and hoping we all make it out alive.

CHAPTER 18
GREY

I pulled Aurelia close and rested my chin on her shoulder.

I hadn't gotten a proper reunion with her, and it was making my wolf even more possessive. He wanted me to kick everyone out of my office and greet her properly.

We had bigger things to deal with, though.

"You have the two shifters in the cells?" I asked Zeke.

"They are, and Erik is in a magicless cell." Zeke stepped forward.

I nodded to him, grateful that he was able to handle all of it while I was getting my mate back.

"Where is the book?" I asked.

Zeke held up a bag and handed it to me.

They couldn't have found a more secure place for it? I lifted a brow at Zeke, but he just shrugged.

"I've had it the whole time. Do you think anyone in this place would dare to cross me?" Zeke grinned.

Asher boomed, "I would!"

"Fuck off, Ash, you're barely healed." Zeke shook his head.

Aurelia reached up a hand, asking for the bag. Zeke handed it to her easily.

I peered over her shoulder into the bag. Aurelia's brow furrowed as she pulled the book from the bag. Her hands glowed softly.

"This isn't the right book," she whispered.

"What?" I shouted. "How do you know?"

"I'm not sure. I just have a feeling this isn't what we need." Aurelia hung her head.

"Don't feel bad. It's not your fault. It's the fucking shifters' fault," I growled, pulling her in closer to me.

"Are we sure it was the shifters and not the brownie?" Zeke asked.

My fist clenched on the desk. That fucking brownie had been the bane of my existence since I'd met him.

"Brownie?" Aurelia asked. "The one from Malcolm's house? How?"

"Yes." I nodded into her shoulder. "I came across him when we were looking for the book."

"He's a mean little thing." She shivered.

Of course. She had encountered him when Malcolm had abducted her.

"That he is, but I wish you'd heard him squeal when I picked him up by his jacket and carried him out of the burning house." I grinned against her shoulder.

"Maybe he didn't know he was grabbing the wrong book?" she asked.

"I'm guessing so, but why did Malcolm destroy my penthouse if he had the correct book?" I stared up at Zeke.

"Maybe we should go ask our little friend that question." Zeke grinned and turned for the door.

I picked up Aurelia as I stood and set her back on her feet. "Let's go have a chat with an asshole brownie."

Aurelia nodded and stepped forward. She had no idea where she was going. I wrapped an arm around her waist and led her to the elevator.

She leaned her head on my chest with a sigh.

"What are we going to do?" she whispered. "We still don't have the right book."

"We'll figure it out," I said as the elevator door opened.

We made our way down to the cells and Karma screamed, "Let me fucking out of here!"

"Shut up, bitch!" I barked as we moved past her.

Aurelia scowled at the woman.

"Oh, you got your princess back," Karma sneered.

"She doesn't know when to shut her fucking mouth," Aurelia mumbled.

Magic sparked along her fingers, but she quickly let it drop. She glared at Karma.

"You'll get your shot at her," I promised, wrapping an arm around my mate.

We stood outside the brownie's cell as we waited for Zeke to open the door. The little shit was huddled in the corner on the small mattress.

"What do you want?" he asked, glaring up at us. His eyes scanned our faces until they landed on the shadow king. His eyes widened and he scrambled to kneel on the floor. "Your Majesty," he spluttered.

"Brownie, where is the real book?" the king asked.

The brownie glanced up with a frown. "His people took it from me." The brownie pointed an accusing finger at me.

"The book they had was not the correct book." I shook my head.

"The wrong book?" the brownie shrieked. His eyes widened and he jumped to his feet.

"I could tell immediately," Aurelia said.

"Burned, burned. The book is burned now!" he wailed, gripping his head.

"What is he babbling about?" Aurelia asked with a shocked gasp.

"Malcolm's home was in flames when we escaped." I scrubbed a hand over my face.

"I barely got to the book before the flames got too big, then the wolf grabbed me and stuck me here." The brownie glared at me.

"So, the book is gone?" Aurelia whispered.

"It can't be, but it doesn't make any sense to me. Why would Malcolm search the penthouse for the book if he still has it?" I asked.

"Maybe he doesn't have it," Aurelia said with wide eyes.

"Did he ever really have it?" I asked.

Zeke ran a hand through his hair. "What book do we have then? It was magical. The princess' magic glowed when she touched it."

"Did Malcolm ever really have the right book?" Aurelia frowned.

Did Aurelia hide it better than any of us thought and then block her memories? That would be extensive magic for just a child to perform.

"Have you gotten any more of your memories back?" I squeezed her to me.

"Not many. Do you think I'm the one who hid it? Why would I have done that?" Aurelia shook her head.

Fenrick shuffled on his feet. "I don't think we should discuss this here."

He eyed the little jerk warily.

He was right. The brownie was loyal to Malcolm. We couldn't give him any more information.

"What other properties does he have?" I turned to the brownie.

"I only know of the place I have served him," he answered.

That was easy. Why would he be so willing to give us that information? Was it because of the king?

"Okay, let's go." I moved to the door.

Everyone filed out behind me, and we went back to the office. The book was still on the desk, and I moved to it with Aurelia by my side.

"Pick up the book." I nodded to her.

She picked it up, and her hands glowed a bright purple. Her eyes widened as she stared down at the strange sight.

"I think I remember this book," she whispered.

"What do you remember?" I asked. If I spoke softly, maybe it wouldn't break her concentration.

"I just know that I had this book before today. I can't really remember much else." She flopped into the chair in front of my desk.

I leaned over her shoulder as she opened it and cursed. "Are all the pages blank?"

"What do you mean?" Aurelia frowned.

"It's blank," I said.

Fenrick stepped up to the other side of Aurelia. "What's the point of a blank book?"

"You can't see the words?" Aurelia asked.

She trailed a finger over the page from left to right as if there was something there only she could see.

"No, there's nothing there." I turned, waving over the shadow king. "Do you see anything?"

"No, nothing. That is strange. Why can Aurelia see it only?" He scratched his head in confusion.

Zeke leaned over and shook his head as well. Why would he think he could see it?

I figured it could only be read by the Fae, but the king and Fenrick didn't see anything either.

"It must have something to do with the prophecy." I sat down next to her.

"I don't think so." Aurelia leaned further over the book.

"What do you see?" I asked.

Aurelia flipped the page and gasped. "It's me."

"What do you mean?" I leaned over her shoulder again even though I couldn't actually see anything.

"I spelled this book. I wrote in these pages, but how?" She shook her head.

How did she do all of this when she was so young?

My phone buzzed in my pocket, and I pulled it out, seeing Magna's number on the screen.

"Magna, what do you know?" I chuckled.

"Aurelia is there?" she asked, even though she probably knew the answer.

"Yes, but you know that already."

"You're in the office?" she asked.

"You know that too. You're our friendly neighborhood seer, so just come on up since I know you're here." I sat back in my chair.

What was the seer going to tell us now?

This night was dragging on and on. I was tired and wanted a proper reunion with my mate.

I hung up the phone and turned to Aurelia. "Magna is here."

"Of course, she is," Dan chuckled.

Magna walked in minutes later.

"Do you know anything about this?" Aurelia asked the seer.

"I do," she said.

Magna glanced down at the book and mumbled something I didn't catch. The book glowed and words filled the page.

"How did you do that? What have you been keeping from us?" I glared at Magna.

"I have kept many things from you for your own protection, Grey," Magna said with a raised brow.

"Of course." I shook my head.

"I knew you before." Aurelia frowned.

"What?" I turned to her sharply.

"It wasn't time for you to remember yet." Magna shrugged.

She sat in the chair on Aurelia's other side.

"Explain!" I barked, crossing my arms over my chest. What had this woman been planning and for how long?

She'd known Aurelia as a child? How?

"I can see the wheels turning in your head. I found her in an alley as a child. I knew she was special. No matter how hard she tried to hide her wings, she couldn't hide them from me." Magna smiled.

"You were in the alley? Are you the reason I lived with the witch?" Aurelia asked.

Was she getting the answers she had been searching for most of her life? Why hadn't Magna told us all this sooner?

"I am the reason for that. You were so small and freezing, but no matter what I saw, it never went well for all of us if I had kept you with me."

How horrible that must have been for her to see all these possible futures and have to hand a child over to someone who would treat her as a slave instead of lovingly.

That was what the witch had done to her. I gritted my teeth against the memory.

"You knew that she would be sleeping in a closet on the floor." I growled.

"You do not get to condemn me for that, shifter king. We would not be here had I chosen differently." Magna crossed her arms over her chest.

"What do you mean?" Aurelia asked.

"You would not have met, and we would not be in a position

to finally go home." Magna smiled softly. "I'm sorry for your struggles, but the future will be bright."

How can she say that with war on the horizon?
No one is safe.

CHAPTER 19
AURELIA

I sat back against my chair in shock. I knew Magna as a child, and she never told me?

"Did you hide the book we need?" I asked softly.

A hand landed on my shoulder, and I glanced up to find my father's green eyes staring back at me.

"I did not hide the book, you did." Magna shook her head.

"You left my daughter, the princess of the kingdom you once belonged to, with a woman who had her sleep on the floor in a closet?" My father boomed.

"Everything I did was so that we could get to this moment." Magna stood and squared off with him.

"What's so important about this moment?" I asked warily, but Magna just smiled.

"It's a turning point. I can't tell you the details or it may change the timeline."

I covered my face with my hands. I was so tired, and all of this was making it worse. I yawned.

"Do you know where the book is hidden?" I asked.

Magna shook her head. "I refused to let you tell me the location of the book."

Grey sat forward. "Smart. Malcolm could have tortured the information out of you."

"So how are we supposed to find it?" I asked.

I didn't remember anything from my childhood except bits and pieces. I didn't remember Magna finding me in the freezing alley. I only remembered Malcolm.

"This book will jog your memories." Magna tapped the book. "You wrote it to remind yourself."

I stroked a finger over the page it was opened to. I hid the real book and left myself clues in this book?

How was I supposed to figure this all out?

Grey cleared his throat. "It's getting late, and I need time with my mate. I think we should pick this up tomorrow."

Magna opened her mouth to argue but closed it and nodded. "I'll go find a place to settle in."

Everyone filed out of the room to find a place to sleep, and I frowned.

"We're sleeping here?" I asked Grey.

I didn't like or trust this place and I wasn't sure I could rest here.

"The penthouse isn't safe. Malcolm has broken in twice now. I don't want to take that chance again." Grey pulled me up into his arms.

"I get that, I just don't like it here." I laid my head on his chest.

"I know." He ran a hand through my hair.

He pulled me closer and kissed my forehead. Everything felt right when I was with Grey like this. "Where are we sleeping?"

"I don't know how much sleep we'll be getting." Grey chuckled.

He tilted my chin up so I could meet his eyes and placed a tender kiss on my lips that made me shiver.

"I'm truly sorry, my love. I should have told you sooner. About

Dan. About the book. About everything. I promise my intentions were not malicious." He said pressed his lips to mine again.

I ran my hands up his chest and wrapped them around the back of his neck as I went up on my tiptoes, pressing my lips harder to his.

His hands slid down my sides slowly until they gripped my ass. I moaned into his mouth, and he took it as permission to deepen the kiss. His tongue met mine in a heated dance as he lifted me, and I wrapped my legs around his hips.

"Wait, Grey, I need a shower," I said, breaking the kiss.

"I don't care." He growled and nipped at my neck.

The skin tingled where he bit me before. "Grey, I still have blood on me from my escape," I said, but he must not have heard me.

My shifter crashed his lips to mine, cutting off any further protests and I melted into him.

His fingers skated up under my shirt, sliding up my waist to cup my breast. He groaned and spun us around, so my back was against the wall and ground his hips into mine.

His cock was rock-hard against my center, and I squirmed in his arms trying to get friction. I still didn't like the idea of having sex with him covered in blood and grime, but this was wild and primitive.

Something about Grey and his hands on me always made me go crazy with need.

"I missed you so much, Princess," Grey groaned against my neck.

Grey licked at the mark on my neck and my back arched, pressing my breasts into his hand.

"We need a bed," I said and gripped his hair.

"We don't need a bed for me to make you come. I could lay you out on my desk again and lick you until you scream my name." Grey ground his hips into my center.

"Grey." I pulled his head back and crashed my lips to his. His dirty mouth alone had me squirming in his arms.

"What do you want, Princess?" Grey asked against my lips.

"You," I moaned, bucking my hips against his hard cock.

"I was so scared I would never hear you say that again." He rested his forehead against my shoulder.

I ran my fingers through his dark hair, and he shivered in my arms.

"It wasn't until I was in that dungeon that I realized how much I need you," I said softly. "I'm sorry that's what it took to realize that I belong with you."

"I'm sorry too. There was just never a good time to tell you." Grey shook his head.

I covered his mouth with my fingers. "I don't want to talk about this right now."

Grey gripped my ass and moved to the desk. He glanced down at the surface before swiping everything off and onto the floor and set me down on it.

He trailed his fingers up over my ass and around to my waist, leaving goose bumps in his wake. Grey gripped my shirt and pulled it up and over my head. He groaned as he stared down at me.

"Take off your bra and lay back on the desk, Aurelia." Grey demands.

I reached back slowly and unhooked my bra, letting the straps slide down my arms. Grey's eyes glowed with his hunger as I bared myself to him. I leaned back on my elbows on the desk and slowly lowered myself onto it. Grey followed, taking my nipple into his mouth and sucking it hard.

My back arched, pushing my breast further into his mouth. His hand slid down my side to the top of my pants and stroked the skin, making me shiver.

"Oh, fuck, Grey," I whispered.

Grey smiled against my skin before switching and giving the other breast the same attention. "You're gonna scream that before I'm done with you, princess." He reached up and pulled at the waistband of my pants.

I lifted my ass off the desk so he could slip my pants down over my hips.

Grey kissed and licked his way down my body while my hands clenched at my sides. His eyes met mine as he threw my pants down and kneeled on the ground at the end of the desk. He trailed his fingers up my calf to my thigh and pushed my legs apart wider.

Inhaling deeply through his nose, Grey grinned. "You smell like heaven when you're so wet for me."

He kissed my inner thigh before nipping it. My hips bucked up, needing him somewhere else entirely.

"Grey, stop teasing me." I groaned.

"I'm not teasing you, I'm worshipping my queen," he growled.

He licked up my thigh until he reached my seam, then moved to the other leg and gave it the same treatment.

I grabbed his hair in an attempt to pull him up to me where I needed him most. Grey rumbled, grabbing my wrists and pinning them to my sides.

"Don't rush me." He nipped my thigh.

"Grey, please," I begged.

My body tensed as he licked up my slit. My back arched and I clenched my hands against the desk, grabbing the edge to keep myself from reaching out and pulling him toward me.

His tongue circled my clit and tingles raced down my spine. He pushed two fingers inside me and groaned.

"So wet for me, Princess."

"Yes," I moaned as he curled his fingers inside me, hitting that spot that made my toes curl. Stars burst behind my eyes and tingles racked my body as I screamed just the way he said I would.

Grey lapped at my juices, prolonging the orgasm even further.

Crawling up my body, he kissed and nipped the entire way until he got to my mouth. He kissed me punishingly, thrusting his tongue between my lips with a growl.

I could taste myself on his lips, and that alone was enough to make me squirm. I reached for his belt, wanting him just as naked as I was but he batted my hands away.

"Patience, my love." He grinned.

Grey leaned up, pulling the shirt over his head and exposing his tanned, toned chest. I trailed my fingers over his abs and his eyes closed tight.

Grey blew out a ragged breath. "Your hands on me make me want to lose control."

"I like watching you lose control." I grinned.

He pulled my hands off him and trapped them at my sides again. "I need you to keep your hands there."

I pouted, wanting to touch him but he just shook his head and gripped his belt. He dropped his pants and boxers slowly to the ground and kicked off his shoes.

He caressed my hips as he stepped between my legs. I kept my hands at my sides as he pulled me down the desk.

He rubbed his cock along my opening slowly but held himself back.

I wiggled my hips suggestively, and his hand clamped down on my thigh in an almost bruising grip.

"Aurelia, do you need something?" Grey chuckled.

"I need you inside me." I moaned as his cock slid over my clit.

"Grip the desk and don't let go," he commanded.

He spread my legs wide and stared down at me before pushing inside me torturously slowly.

I held onto the desk with a white-knuckle grip, wishing that I could touch him but not wanting him to stop, either.

When he was finally buried deep inside me, Grey scrunched his eyes closed as he blew out a shaky breath. I wiggled my hips, needing him to move again.

Pain and pleasure warred within me as he smacked my ass.

"If that's supposed to be a deterrent, it's not gonna work," I said softly.

"Need a minute. It's been too long, and my wolf is going crazy with his need to reclaim his mate." Grey growled.

When he opened his eyes once more, his pupils glowed with his wolf close to the surface.

Grey circled my clit with his thumb as he pulled out so slowly, I could have screamed. He was fucking torturing me in the best way.

He pushed inside me hard and fast on the next thrust, and my back arched off the desk, spots dancing behind my eyes.

He thrust in again, and I wrapped my legs around his hips to grind myself against him.

"Fuck, Princess, I'm not going to last. Can I mark you?" Grey leaned over me then, crushing his lips down on mine.

I groaned into the kiss, keeping my hands on the desk.

He broke away and kissed and licked across my jaw to the mark on my shoulder and nipped it playfully.

"Yes, Grey," I hissed.

Fangs scraped slowly over my skin, and I shivered, tightening my legs around him and pulling him inside me deeper until he hit that spot.

My head thrashed and pleasure pulsed through me, taking me higher than before as his fangs slid into the mark on my neck.

He roared against my neck as he slammed himself inside me a final time, spilling his hot seed inside of me.

CHAPTER 20
GREY

I rolled over and pulled my mate into my arms, still half-groggy with sleep.

After our fun on the desk the night before, I'd carried her to the bedroom I kept here in case of emergencies and helped her shower before falling into bed.

"We have to get up, don't we?" She yawned.

"Yes, unfortunately. We need to find the place a child would hide a book." I grumbled.

"I don't want to," she said, rolling into me so her head was against my chest.

I didn't want to get up either. I hadn't had nearly enough time with my mate like this, but we needed the book to stop the elders.

"There's no rest for the wicked, love." I grinned and patted her back.

"I'm not wicked," she griped. "I hate that term for Fae."

"I know, Princess. Poor choice of words." I squeezed her to me tighter.

She sighed and sat up in bed, the sheet pooling around her waist making me impossibly hard.

I glanced away, knowing that if I didn't stop staring at her we wouldn't be leaving the bed any time soon.

"What am I going to wear?" She glared at the pile of dirty clothes on the floor.

"I have spare clothing in the closet." I shrugged.

She jumped from the bed naked, and I stared as she crossed the room. I adjusted myself beneath the sheets and sighed. There was no way to just take this time with her.

Time was ticking, even with the book Aurelia wrote to give herself clues. The elders were bound to send more people after her and the book.

We needed a win, desperately.

"You have women's clothes in here." Aurelia peeked her head out of the closet with a raised brow.

"I brought them from the apartment after the first time we were attacked by Malcolm just in case." I got up from the bed and moved toward the dresser.

I pulled black jeans from the drawer and unfolded them before putting them on. I paused when a knock sounded on the door. I turned to make sure that Aurelia was dressed before stomping to answer it.

I threw the door open to find Dan there, his back straight and his eyes wide with panic.

"What's wrong?" I barked.

The acrid scent of his fear hit me in the gut as he glanced away.

"Someone is tampering with the wards." He fidgeted, moving from foot to foot.

"Have you sent a team out?" I moved to the closet to grab a shirt.

Aurelia stood there with wide eyes.

"We have, but the person will only speak to the princess. Alone." Dan scrubbed a hand over his face.

"Absolutely not," I growled.

"I figured you would say that." Dan sighed.

"Why does he want to speak to me?" Aurelia stepped out of the closet.

"He didn't say." Dan said shaking his head.

"It could be anyone, Aurelia." I turned, pulling her into me.

"What if it's Malcolm with Freya?" she gasped.

Fuck. What if it was Malcolm? We didn't have the book we needed.

"Then we trade him the brownie." I crossed my arms over my chest.

"Are we sure that's a good idea?" Aurelia asked, chewing her lip. "He heard a lot yesterday."

"We don't have another choice. We don't have the book, and have no idea where it is," I said.

"Agreed, and he can't have the book we have. It may be the only clue we have on the actual book." Dan leaned against the door frame.

"Maybe we can wait. It may not even be Malcolm." Aurelia laid her head on my shoulder.

She hated this. Freya was once again in the hands of a monster, and she just wanted her back. I squeezed her tighter to me and glanced back to Dan.

"Get everyone together in the conference room. We're going to take a look." I stepped toward Dan, who was blocking the door.

"Are you sure that's wise, boss?" Dan scratched his head.

"I can't have people tampering with my wards." I stomped out, pulling Aurelia with me.

Maybe I should have left her with Dan and checked for myself.

I pushed the button for the elevator and waited. When the doors opened, the shadow king was inside.

"Where are you going?" KingChanning asked.

"Someone is screwing with the wards. I need to check it out." I moved into the elevator, Aurelia following closely behind me.

"Why are you going, daughter? You should stay here. I'll go with your king." The shadow king clapped me on the shoulder.

"The person wants to speak to me," she said, staring straight ahead.

"All the more reason for you to stay behind." The king growled.

"I'm an adult and can take care of myself." Aurelia stomped her foot.

"I'm going with her, and we are staying on our side of the wards." I pulled Aurelia into my side and kissed her temple.

"I'm going too," King Channing insisted.

He leaned back against the wall of the elevator, and I pushed the button for the parking garage.

When we got to the parking garage several supernaturals were standing around, their expressions shuttered.

"Where are they?" I asked, stepping closer.

A shifter was pushed forward, glancing down in submission.

"Boss, he was adamant it only be the princess." His fear permeated the air.

"I don't care what he was adamant about." I shook my head.

Whoever he was, I wasn't leaving my mate alone with him, especially with so many threats against her.

"He's screwing with the wards at the road leading to the city." Another shifter pointed over his shoulder.

I nodded to the shifter, and marched past him with the king and Aurelia at my back. Someone clapped me on the shoulder and the world spun around.

Motherfucker. I was not expecting that.

"You can't just do that without warning," I spat at the king as we appeared at the edge of the wards.

He wasn't paying attention to me. His eyes blazed with fury as he stared at someone behind me.

I spun around and growled as my wolf beat at the cage in my chest. Ronaldo stood on the other side of my wards with a smug-as-fuck smile on his face.

"What the fuck do you want?" I snarled.

"The princess is condemned to death. I'm here to take my prisoner back to be punished for her crimes." He shrugged.

"You have no jurisdiction here. Fuck off!" I yelled.

"I don't?" Ronaldo asked.

What the fuck was he talking about? Of course, he didn't. We weren't in Faery. I hadn't been back in two centuries.

It was my sole mission to return my people there and my mate was going to help me do it. I refused to give her to this bastard elder to be executed.

"No, this is my property, and you are trespassing. Leave." I turned my back on the elder.

The man growled at the slight. Turning my back on him was a major disrespect to him. I didn't give a shit.

"You will give the princess to me before all is said and done. Her real betrothed misses her terribly." Ronaldo smiled.

"Real betrothed?" Aurelia scoffed.

"Malcolm will pay for the things he's done!" the shadow king roared.

"He's baiting you, Shadow King," I said, gripping his shoulder.

I tightened my arm around Aurelia as she glared at the elder.

"I will never be with Malcolm!" Aurelia yelled.

"Shhh, I know. Don't let the old fool rile you up, my love." I shook my head.

I would die before I let that bastard touch her again. She was mine. My wolf snarled in my mind at just the thought of her being with anyone else.

Another man stepped forward, and I jumped in front of the shadow king. "I know how badly you want to kill him, but don't go out there."

Aurelia crossed her arms over her chest and glared at Malcolm. "Where is Freya?"

"Nothing he says is going to be true." I pulled her away.

"Where is my brownie and my book your lover stole?" Malcolm sneered.

"Do not speak to her!" the king roared.

This was devolving quickly and if I didn't hold the king back, we would have someone else to save from Malcolm.

"You want your brownie, give me Freya. The book never belonged to you. It was Aurelia's." I turned back to the assholes.

"No," Malcolm growled.

"Fine," I said with a shrug. "I'll keep the brownie. You left him in a fiery inferno anyway."

"I want the book!" he roared.

He beat on the wards but was unable to pass them. No one with ill intent could get through them. A very powerful witch set them up for me long ago.

"You're not getting that book," Aurelia hissed.

She crossed her arms over her chest and planted her feet.

"I can make you give me the book." A malicious grin spread over Malcolm's face as he pulled something from his pocket.

Aurelia gasped as he pulled Freya from his pocket in a tight fist. Her hands crackled with magic.

Freya's limp form made me see red and my wolf snarled in my mind. He pushed at my restraints. He wanted to tear the man apart for so many reasons.

Aurelia launched the magic at him through the wards. He dove out of the way with a roar. His hand opened and Freya went flying.

I didn't think, just reacted, barreling through the ward to catch her before she hit the ground and did even more damage.

Ronaldo shouted something and I dove out of the way as he threw electricity at me. I landed in a heap next to Freya and scooped her up into my hand.

"Grey?" she mumbled.

"I've got you," I whispered.

"Die, shifter king!" Ronaldo roared, and a scream tore through the air.

Lightning crashed into the ground around us but didn't hit me as I rolled to my feet at the same time Malcolm launched himself at me.

I turned fast, elbowing him in the gut. A crunch sounded and I grinned as he bellowed in pain. I rolled away, back to the edge of the wards as excruciating pain tore through my back.

"Aurelia!" I shouted and tossed Freya to her on the other side of the wards as I fell to my knees.

Electricity tore through me, and my body twitched as I fell face down, half inside the wards.

The shadow king bellowed, his shadows lashing out at the men on the other side of the wards. He directed them to me, pulling me back inside the wards with a huff.

"Grey," Aurelia said and dropped to her knees next to me.

Her hands ran down my body and over my back. Healing magic pulsed between us, but I stared up at her in question.

Aurelia grinned and nodded to Freya, who was safely resting on our side of the ward.

"You did it. You got her back." Aurelia grinned.

"Good. We didn't even have to give him anything." I collapsed to the dirt road with a groan.

"Maybe we finally have a win," she whispered, but turned at her father's shout of rage.

"Come back, cowards!" King Channing roared.

Malcolm and Ronaldo sifted away, knowing they were beaten and no longer had anything to bargain with.

I rolled to stare at Freya again. She was so small and fragile. I just wanted to protect her, always. She'd been with me forever.

She had to be okay. Fiona would be devastated if anything happened to her. I would be devastated.

She was family and always would be. I could not bear the loss of her.

CHAPTER 21
Aurelia

"Someone help!" I yelled as we ran into the infirmary.

Grey cradled Freya's tiny body close as we ran. It would have been touching if I wasn't so scared for the sprite.

A healer peeked out of a room with wide eyes and beckoned us forward. "We don't have the right healing for sprites, sir."

"We need Magna," I said.

Where was she? She always seemed to pop up whenever we needed her.

"She should be in my office, I think," Grey said and turned back to the elevator.

"I'll go get her." I raced to the elevator and stabbed at the button.

Freya was my friend, and this was the second time she'd been harmed because of me. I would make Malcolm pay before this was all over.

The doors opened on the top floor, and I rushed down the hall to Grey's office. The door flew open at my approach and Asher stood there his arms crossed over his chest.

"What's happened?" he asked.

"I need Magna. Freya is in bad shape." I brushed passed him.

"You got her back?" Asher followed me into the office.

I scanned the faces in the office but there was no sign of her.

"We did but she isn't doing good. Where is Magna?"

Fenrick stepped forward and placed a hand on my arm. "Calm down, Princess. Take me to her, I can help."

"You can?" I asked hopefully.

"I have healing abilities just like I imagine you will once you practice." Fenrick patted my arm.

"I already have some." I didn't have time for him to placate me, I spun on my heel and ran down the hall. Rushed steps followed behind me as I stopped at the elevator and jabbed my finger into the button.

Asher stepped next to me. "We'll get her fixed up, Aurelia."

"How can you be so sure? You didn't see her." Tears stung the backs of my eyes.

"She's the strongest little sprite I've ever seen. She'll make it through this." Asher grinned.

The elevator doors opened, and we stepped inside. I pushed the button repeatedly for the floor of the infirmary.

Shuffling my feet, I stood there waiting impatiently for the damn doors to open.

The doors opened and I moved to rush out, but a hand on my shoulder stopped me. I glanced up at the numbers and huffed.

Wrong floor. Shit.

"Aurelia, I'm here for Freya." Magna said, stepping into the elevator.

I collapsed into the other woman's arms with a sob, grateful we'd found her. Freya needed her desperately.

She patted my back as the elevator doors closed behind her.

"She's really hurt!" I cried.

"We will do all we can," Magna soothed.

The elevator arrived at the correct floor, and I straightened my shoulders. I swiped at the tears on my cheeks and strode into the sterile hall.

Father nodded his head to a door at the end, and I dragged Magna to it. I knocked on the door before pushing it open, too impatient to care about manners right then.

Grey's face softened when he saw me, and he opened his arms for me to step into his strength. Magna rushed to Freya, her hands glowing green.

I rested my head on my shifter's chest, praying to whatever gods were listening that the tiny sprite would be okay.

"We are no good to her here." Grey squeezed me tightly. "We need to find that book before the elders do."

I nodded. He was right. Magna could handle healing Freya, and she would be good as new soon.

Grey led me from the room with an arm around my shoulder, my father and Asher following behind.

I had been in a daze the whole elevator ride hoping Magna would be able to heal poor Freya. Her tiny, broken body would haunt me much like when Fiona was injured at Malcolm's house of horrors.

We walked into the office, Zeke and Dan sitting in the chairs in front of the desk. Someone must have cleaned Grey's office because everything was back in its place.

I couldn't even bring myself to blush about what had happened there the night before.

Zeke smirked but quickly dropped it at the expression on my face.

"What happened?" he asked.

"Malcolm and Ronaldo were at the wards with Freya." Grey sighed.

"The elders know where to find us now. They probably

wanted to talk to me alone because I would have traded myself for Freya. I've done it before." I ran a hand down my face.

"All we can do now is look for the real book and hope Magna can heal her." Grey squeezed me tighter to him and led me to the chair behind the desk.

He sat in the chair and pulled me down in his lap possessively. I reached for the book and pulled it into my arms before opening it.

Grey rested his chin on my shoulder, reading the book with me. Where the hell did child me hide the damn book? Would I even be able to find it without my memories?

"I don't know if this is even going to have the answers we need." I shook my head.

"Why not?" Grey asked, kissing my cheek.

"I went to a lot of trouble to make sure no one could find it. I even blocked my own memories to accomplish it. Magna easily broke the spell on it so others could see what it said."

"So, you think you need to unlock your memories?" Grey asked. "That didn't go so well the last time."

"I went through that block like a freight train, and I still didn't retrieve everything," I agreed.

"Maybe there's an answer you need in the book." Grey squeezed me.

I glanced back down at the words. How did I write in such a beautiful, curling script at such a young age? How was it even possible.

I turned the page and gasped, my mind spinning with memories.

I ran through the forest outside the castle giggling wildly as someone chased me.

"Princess, don't run from me. How am I supposed to protect you if you're constantly running way?" Fenrick's panicked voice made me giggle more and I ran faster.

"You're supposed to catch me, silly." I ran into the hollow of a tree and hid as he passed.

I giggled again as I ran the other direction, away from Fenrick. He was stuffy and never wanted to let me play.

Running into the stables, I hid in one of the stalls with Buttercup. I backed into the corner and plastered myself there, so Fenrick couldn't find me.

Voices filled the space and I strained to listen. It wasn't Fenrick. Malcolm was talking to someone quietly. "You know what will happen if we do this," he said to someone I couldn't see.

"You must. She is too dangerous to be here. If she knew what she is capable of, she could overthrow everything we have built here. Our plans for both realms could be ruined," the man whispered.

I didn't recognize his voice, but it sounded familiar.

"The king will hunt me down if I do this." Malcolm growled.

"Then dump the girl in the first major city. She won't be able to take care of herself. Maybe she'll die, and it will save us the trouble of having to kill her later."

Who were they talking about? Why would they want to kill a girl? It didn't make any sense.

Heavy footsteps came into the stable, and I peeked out through the slats. Malcolm and the man were gone. Fenrick stood on the other side of the stall, and I breathed a sigh of relief.

I didn't think it would be good for them to see me when they were plotting someone's death. Who were they going to kill, and why would Daddy hunt him down for it?

I peeked out of the stall and Fenrick frowned when he saw the expression on my face.

"What is it, Princess?" he asked.

"How did you find me?" I stomped my foot.

He crouched in front of me with a frown. "This is one of your favorite places to hide. Of course, I found you here."

I shook my head to clear the memory. Everyone in the room

was staring at me with matching frowns on their faces. Grey gripped my chin and turned me to face him.

"What happened? I called your name several times," he said.

"I remembered something. I was running from Fenrick and hid in the stables. Malcolm was talking to someone. I'm pretty sure it was Ronaldo." I grimaced.

"You never told me about that." Fenrick crossed his arms over his chest.

"That's not the point." I waved him off. "Is it possible that I made it back through the portal as a child and hid the book there?"

"That doesn't make any sense, though." Grey shook his head. "Why would you come back? You were cold and alone in most of the visions you have seen."

"I don't know, but I have a feeling the other book has something to do with it." I rubbed at my temples.

Why was that memory attached to this book? It has to be important, but how?

"What did Malcolm say?" Fenrick growled.

"They were talking about my abduction and inevitable death." I shook my head.

"While you hid in a stall," Fenrick said softly.

I nodded. There wasn't much more to say. As a child, I hadn't known who they had been talking about, but after what happened in my life, they were definitely talking about killing me.

"Malcolm tried to play me into thinking he was protecting me from the Council, but since I overheard that conversation, I already knew he was lying. So why did I go with him in the first place?"

The more I knew, the less I understood. Every time I learned something, I just had more questions.

I turned my attention back to the book, running my fingers along the swooping letters.

Fenrick cleared his throat. "Maybe we should check the stables."

"I need to know for sure," I said, not looking up from the book. "It doesn't make sense why I would go and then come back, especially when I remembered the life I had there."

"Keep reading." Grey nudged me. "You might remember more."

I glanced back down at the book, reading the words, but no new memories came to me. Turning the page, I frowned.

"It's some kind of map?" I asked, showing Grey.

Grey shook his head. "I can't see it."

"What? Magna already took the enchantment off the book." I peered down at the hand-drawn map in the book with a frown.

"Maybe this is a different enchantment. Magna might not know about it." Grey frowned.

Fenrick stood and walked over, staring at the book in my lap but shook his head as well.

"I don't see anything either," Fenrick grumbled.

"Is it a map to the book?" I frowned.

I turned the book sideways, but couldn't figure out what it was a map of at all. "We need Magna, but I don't want to disturb her while she's working on Freya."

"In the meantime, can you draw it so we can see it?" Grey asked.

"Maybe. I don't know. I was a child when I drew this. I didn't even know I could draw." I set the book back on the desk.

"You were always drawing me pictures." Father grinned.

Grey opened a drawer in the desk and pulled out a stack of papers and a pencil and set them on the desk next to the book.

I really hoped I could do this. It could be the only way to go forward to stop the elders.

They had plans for both realms, and I shuddered to think what those plans would mean for the rest of us.

CHAPTER 22
GREY

"**A**rgh!" Aurelia yelled and slammed the pencil down on the desk.

"Is it not working?" I glanced over her shoulder.

"It keeps moving. Every time I try to draw something, it moves. I don't think it's going to let me draw it. I need to learn more." She placed her head in her hands.

"Can you read anything else on there? Any idea what it is?" I rubbed her shoulders.

She was tense but I would have been too. It wasn't fair that this was all on her shoulders. We were mates. She should have been able to lean on me.

"No, nothing sounds familiar to me." She shook her head.

"Read it. Maybe one of us will know," I said.

"Motherfucker!" she screamed. "All the letters are scrambled now."

What the hell kind of enchantment did she put on this map that she couldn't share it with anyone?

"Maybe keep reading the other pages? It might help." I patted her shoulder.

Dan rushed into the office and waved a hand at me. I walked out to him, frowning as he held out his phone to me. A video was queued to play.

I played the video and cursed. It was grainy, obviously from a surveillance camera. But a man had shifted into a wolf in full view of the camera and attacked someone. The video cut out to a news story.

"Where was this taken?" I asked with a growl.

"Right here in Dallas. On the shifter side." Dan gritted his teeth.

"Is there a way we can spin this? Debunk it as Photoshop or something?" I ran a hand down my face.

"It's already everywhere. The guy is in the human jail."

"How the fuck did the human police catch a damn shifter?" I groaned.

This was the last thing we needed piled on top of everything else.

"They had to have help. There's no way a human, or even multiple humans, could take down a shifter." Dan shuffled his feet warily.

"There's gotta be a way to get the guy out of jail. He's going to end up in a fucking lab somewhere." I clenched my fist, wanting desperately to punch something.

How could one of my shifters be so stupid? Our entire existence for centuries was a highly guarded secret.

Zeke turned to us with a scowl. "What's going on?"

"Fucking shifter went wolf on someone and it was caught on a security camera," I growled.

Zeke pulled his phone from his pocket and typed something into it. He frowned down at the screen.

"It says a bystander subdued the wolf with magic." Zeke tilted his head back.

"What the fuck?" I hollered. "Does it say anything about the location of the bystander? Who the fuck would openly use magic in front of humans?"

I turned at Aurelia's gasp.

"What is it?" I asked, spinning to face her.

Was she having another memory? Did she find something out about the book?

"Something they said in the memory. They have plans for both realms. Could this be it? Are they trying to out us to the humans so they will eradicate us?" Aurelia sat back in the chair.

"It's probably more nefarious than that, but I bet I know someone who has some answers." I grinned, waving to Dan and Zeke to follow me.

"Where are you going?" Aurelia asked.

"Going to have a chat. Stay with the book. Fenrick will keep watch." I jogged from the office to the elevator.

Fenrick nodded. He had been her protector as a child and had guarded her so far. I trusted him to watch her back.

"Who are we going to chat with?" Zeke asked as he came up beside me.

"Who else but their spy would know the Council's plans?" I smiled grimly.

"You think Erik will tell us anything even if he does know?" Zeke pushed the button to the elevator.

"I'm not going to give him a choice." I stepped inside the elevator and pushed the button as the men followed behind me.

"He's a Council spy, so he's adept at torture," Zeke said as the elevator dinged.

I stepped out of the elevator and on cue, Karma started screaming from her cell.

"Shut the fuck up!" I roared.

The bitch was asking for execution if she didn't stop annoying the fuck out of me.

"What are you going to do to me?" Karma yelled.

I'd had enough. The bitch didn't know when to quit. I stormed to her cell and grasped her by the throat through the bars.

"I said shut up. You sold us out. You're lucky you're sitting in a cell, and I didn't throw you in the enchanted ring the way Layla went out." I squeezed her throat.

Her eyes widened as she gasped for breath. She reached up to claw at my hand, and I tossed her away. Her back hit the bars on the other side of the cell with a thud.

I spun on my heel and stormed down the hall of cells. Erik was in a cell in the back of the hall, away from all other prisoners.

It blocked magic just as the brownie's cell, did but I was cautious about opening the door. Erik was cunning and much larger than the brownie. He was also skilled in combat even without magic.

"Be vigilant. He may try to rush us when we open the door," I said over my shoulder.

Zeke and Dan nodded. I rolled my shoulders and grabbed the key from my pocket. It was the master key to all the cells. I was the only person in possession of one.

"Stay back from the door, Erik!" I shouted through the door before sliding the key card in the lock and opening the door with a click.

Erik sat back on the cot with a smug grin on his stupid face. I stormed in and the door clicked shut behind us as Dan and Zeke followed.

"What do the elders want with the human realm?" I crossed my arms over my chest.

Erik shrugged one shoulder but kept his mouth shut. I glared at the Fae and took a threatening step forward.

"What are you going to do, Grey? Torture me? Good luck." Erik laughed, shaking his head.

"Do you know who I am?" Zeke stepped forward.

Was he about to use his rider powers on the Fae?

Erik gulped. He nodded, and the bravado slipped from his face.

"Not so tough now then?" I raised my brows.

Zeke laughed. "You know I can show you your worst nightmares and feast on your soul while I'm doing it."

"It's why you were exiled, criminal. The hunt was barbaric." Erik sneered.

"You're gonna tell us what you know, Erik, or you will be the next victim of the wild hunt." I shrugged.

In the end it wasn't up to me, but Asher would take my request into consideration and most likely would run the fucker down in the forest of Faery when Aurelia and I got us back home.

We were going to get us all home, especially now that the humans knew about us.

"I won't betray the Council." Erik spat.

I turned to Zeke and nodded.

"Did the Council out us to the humans?" I asked.

Zeke gripped Erik by the chin and stared into his eyes. It only took a second before the man started screaming and thrashing.

Erik closed his eyes tightly, but the nightmare was already playing out.

Zeke straightened and crossed his arms over his chest.

The screams died down and we waited. It did no good to try to ask questions while he was hollering because he was in his own head.

"Zeke is a scary motherfucker," Dan whispered next to me.

"Yeah, so maybe think twice before you shoot a woman with a tranquillizer dart in the future," Zeke muttered.

Sounded like everyone was angry over that particular revelation.

"I'm going to ask again, Erik. Did the Council out magic to the humans?" I asked.

Muddy brown eyes turned to me and he nodded.

"What is their end game here?" I asked.

Erik braced himself for pain and shook his head.

Fuck. He wasn't going to give us anything. He would rather live his worst nightmares over and over than give us anything more.

"We should just talk to Ash. Once we go home, you can hunt him in the wild as you used to." I shrugged and turned to leave.

"You mean to go back?" Erik frowned.

"Yes, we are going home," I growled. "Leave him here and you can do what you want to punish him once we take down the elders."

"I really want to give him another nightmare." Zeke chuckled.

"Do what you will." I waved a hand over my shoulder. "If he gives you any more information, let me know."

I walked out of the cell and down the hall. Karma was blessedly silent. Dan followed closely behind me, and I turned to him after pushing the button for the elevator.

"Send a team to investigate the human jail. Someone has to be able to get the man out of there before he's taken by the human authorities and tested," I said.

The elevator doors opened, and I stepped inside. Dan had his nose in his phone as he typed away on it.

"Got it, boss. I'll have our best team on it now." Dan never glanced up from his phone.

"Do you even know who the best team is?" I sighed.

"I've been going through files in my office. I take my job seriously," he said, affronted.

"Good." I leaned back against the wall, anxious to get back up to my office.

I hated having to wait in the elevator. If only I could sift like the Fae. I could just pop into my office, but not only was it not an ability shifters had, but I placed wards against sifting within the building.

The doors opened and shouting came from my office, the noise carrying down the hall. I didn't even think about, I just sprinted down the corridor to my open office door.

Fenrick was standing over my mate, her eyes wide and unseeing. I pushed the Fae away from her and snatched her up from the chair.

Her heart was beating wildly in my ears with my shifter hearing. "She's alive, I just don't know what's happening."

"Is she having a vision?" Fenrick asked in shock.

Why would he be shocked? Fae often had the gift of sight. She could very well have that gift. We had yet to uncover everything Aurelia could do with her magic.

"Maybe? I don't know. I've never seen her do this," I said.

"She already has so many gifts. This could make her an even bigger target," Fenrick whispered.

I squeezed her to me. It wasn't her fault she was chosen or had all this power.

"Maybe it was something to do with the book?" I asked hopefully.

"It's possible that it was the book. She was reading it when her eyes rolled back in her head." Fenrick shook his head.

"What could she possibly be seeing? What is in that blasted book?" I growled as I sat with her in the chair behind my desk.

I ran my hand through her hair and kissed her forehead. "Wake up, my love. Wake up."

She twitched a bit in my arms and moaned softly.

"Grey?" she mumbled. "I know what they are doing and where to find the book."

CHAPTER 23
AURELIA

Magna smiled softly as she caressed the book. "You must hide this, child."

"Where?" I chewed my lip.

I didn't know any safe places in the human realm. I only just found someone kind enough to take me in. Where could I possibly hide it?

"No one can know, not even you, until the time is right. The elders have terrible plans and if we don't do things exactly right, we could doom us all." Magna sat back in her armchair.

"No pressure," I mumbled.

She reached up and patted my hand. "You must hide it where they least suspect it."

They would never expect it to be at home. Could I go back just for a minute and hide it in one of my usual hiding places?

Mommy and Daddy must be so sad. If I had known that Malcolm and that man were talking about me, then I would have told someone of their plans. I would have warned them or told Fenrick.

Magna said it's better that I didn't. That future didn't turn out the way it was supposed to.

"How do I get to the portal?" I asked.

"No one has seen the portal in centuries." She shook her head.

"I was brought through the portal into the forest." I fidgeted, twisting my fingers together.

Magna closed her eyes briefly but opened them with a snap. She moved to a book on the shelf and pulled a different book off.

She flipped through the book and grimaced. "You're going to need to use this enchantment, child."

She handed me the book that was written in Fae and I cocked my head to the side.

"If I do this, how will I ever know where it's hidden?" I asked, peering up at the woman.

"You won't remember until the time is right. I know I am putting a lot on your small shoulders, but I promise it's for a good cause. You will be happy one day and our people—all of them—will prosper."

"I just want to go home. I won't even run and hide from Fenrick anymore if I can just go home." My lip wobbled.

"I know." She rubbed my back. "It's not a good idea right now though."

"What happens if I go home and stay there and forget this world even exists?" I sniffled. I peered up to her with pleading eyes. Why couldn't I just go home? Was it really that bad?

"If you go back and stay there, you will die," she said in a low voice.

Her words rang with truth. I gasped and stared down at the enchantment in the book she'd handed me.

Was she telling the truth or trying to scare me to do what she wanted me to?

"You've seen my death?" I asked in a small voice.

"A million different ways," she mumbled, glancing away.

"I don't want to die." I straightened my shoulders.

I would do what needed to be done. I would suffer if I had to. I had already suffered the cold and loneliness. How hard could it be?

"I know, Princess. I don't want you to die either. It's why we have to be very careful." She turned away as if to collect her thoughts and sighed.

I picked up the golden book and stood, making my way to Magna. "Can you sift?"

"Yes, I can." She nodded. "Where do you need me to go?"

I thought hard about the place we'd come out in the portal all those months ago, and Magna turned curious eyes on me.

"I thought you understood." She crossed her arms over her chest.

"I do. I'm not going to stay there. I am very good at sneaking around the palace grounds." I squeezed her arm.

Magna nodded and then we were swirling through space and time to the shimmering portal.

"C'mon," I said, waving her to the portal.

"I can't come with you, Princess. No one can know what you do with that book. I must remember some things about you but not all." She took a step back.

"Will you be here when I come back?" I asked.

"I will see it when you come back but I fear staying here too long." She glanced around the clearing as if she was waiting for someone to jump out at us.

Maybe she was.

"Okay, I'll be back." I took a step toward the shimmering portal with a small amount of trepidation before taking a deep breath and going through.

Cool water washed over me as I stepped into the glittering portal, but I was dry when I got to the other side. The forest in the palace grounds greeted me like an old friend.

Tree branches reached out in welcome. A gust of wind nearly pushed me back and I scanned the forest.

A new urgency fell over the forest that made me tense. The trees were urging me to move. They wanted me to hide.

I ran to a huge oak and just like a lot of the times I played and hid from Fenrick a hollow opened up in the center. I ducked *inside and bushes moved in front hiding me from whoever was coming.*

"The king suspects it was me," Malcolm said angrily.

"Yes, I fear what he will do when he has proof." It was the same voice as before.

I peeked over the bushes and my eyes widened when I saw Ronaldo the elder with squinty eyes standing in front of Malcolm.

Why was he there? What did he have to gain from my death? Our elders were supposed to be wise. Why would I be a threat?

"How do we stop him from seeing the truth?" Malcolm growled.

"We do not. You must stay in the human world to keep watch over the girl from afar. She has something we need. If you can convince her to work with us to take over the human world and make the others our slaves as they should be, even better." Ronaldo shrugged.

I nearly gasped but covered it quickly. They wanted to rule both realms? But why? They were already the most powerful in Faery, so what good would it do them to rule the humans too?

"If I can convince her to help us, she doesn't have to die, right? I can keep my betrothed," Malcolm asked with a relieved sigh.

"Fine, fine. Now get back to the human realm. Keep an eye on the princess and find the book." Ronaldo waved a dismissive hand and sifted away.

I blinked away the memory. Strong arms were wrapped around my body, and I stared into the beautiful eyes of my mate.

"Grey?" I mumbled. "I know what they are doing and where to find the book."

"My love, you scared the life out of me and poor Fenrick." He squeezed me tighter to him.

"I'm okay. I poured my memories into that book. All of the most dangerous ones to us were put there." I wiggled in his arms.

He didn't loosen his hold, instead he sat in his chair with me cradled in his lap.

"What did you see?" Fenrick asked.

"I went back to Faery once, but I had to block out the memories or someone would be able to find it." I shook my head.

"You hid the book in Faery?" Grey asked, defeated.

Why was he defeated? I could just bring him through the portal with me.

"I didn't know the human realm. I thought that was the best place. No one would think a child would be strong enough to get themselves back home and then leave willingly, but the threat was clear." I shrugged as best I could in his tight embrace.

"You hid it in the very last place anyone would expect. Right under their noses. There's just one problem, Princess." Fenrick flopped into the chair across from us.

"What?" I asked with a frown.

What was I missing? It was all so simple. Go to the forest get the book and come back.

"You can't sift at all, not to mention between realms, and the portal is watched closely by the elders." Fenrick leaned forward on his elbows.

"Fuck," I said and ran a hand down my face.

He was right. I wouldn't be able to bring anyone else if my father or someone sifted me there. Grey wouldn't be able to come with me. Would two warriors be enough if the Council guards found us?

My thoughts raced back to Nickolas and his death. We had only a few soldiers with us, and we were still in trouble. I'd lost a friend that day.

A tear leaked from my eye and rolled down my cheek, but Grey wiped it away.

"It's okay, love. We'll figure out a way to get the book. Don't get upset," Grey whispered and kissed my forehead.

He thought I was crying because of the book? It was difficult but not impossible to get. I was remembering the blood and Nickolas' dying request.

Fenrick stared at me from across the desk.

"You said you knew what the elders are up to?" he asked.

"It's terrible and I'm not even sure if it's too late to stop them." I chewed my lip.

I patted Grey's arm, and he reluctantly let me sit up but didn't take his arms from around my waist.

"What is it?" Grey frowned.

"They want to enslave everyone, including the humans."

Fenrick stood abruptly, his hands clenched in anger.

"They're mad. The humans will wipe the Fae off the planet. They have weapons and technology that we don't, and the sheer numbers alone far outmatch us." He ran a shaky hand through his hair.

"That is a suicide mission." Grey's hands clenched my hips roughly.

"I don't know how long they have been plotting this. They could already have their plan in motion." I leaned my head back on Grey's shoulder and stared up at the ceiling.

"The shifter," Grey said. "They are behind it."

I nodded because that was probably true. They were probably infiltrating the human world for a long time. Setting everything in motion to enslave all the people they perceived as weaker than them.

"What do we do?" I asked.

"I have a team going to rescue the shifter from the human jail as we speak. They will get him out and then we find out what happened to make the idiot shift." Grey shook his head.

Fenrick's eyes blazed with fury. "Then we get the book and find a way to stop them."

Dan ran into the room, his breathing shallow, as if he'd run up the stairs instead of taking the elevator.

"The team is back. They have the shifter in holding," he said through wheezing breaths.

"That was quicker than I expected." Grey stood with me in his arms.

I wiggled until he put me down. His arm snaked around my waist as he rushed to the door.

"I had already sent them when you asked. I didn't want to tell you because I wasn't sure how you would react." Dan's cheeks turned pink.

"Good instincts. We don't want our people coming up missing or being experimented on." Grey clapped him on the shoulder.

We raced to the holding floor, unsure what we were going to find. The team that Dan assembled stood in the hall ragged, and a couple were bleeding.

"Report!" Grey barked.

The three men glanced between each other warily and shuffled their feet nervously. What was so concerning that they were afraid to speak?

The one in the middle stepped forward. He had magic. There was a subtle buzz of it around him.

He bowed his head in submission. "This was not your average jail break, boss. We barely made it out alive."

"Explain," Grey ordered.

His hand tensed on my thigh.

"That wasn't a human jail. The guards had magic. Every last one of them."

CHAPTER 24
GREY

"The fuck did you say?" I growled.

That was a typical human jail. How the fuck did a bunch of supernaturals get in there?

"It wasn't normal magic, boss. It was stronger and different from mine," the guy said.

"They're Fae?" Aurelia asked with wide eyes.

She turned to stare at me in horror. Why on earth would they take over the human jails when we had our own ways of dealing with our people?

"How long have they been here?" I asked, but no one had the answers.

I still needed to talk with the shifter. Find out how he'd become the Council's target. How they made him shift in front of the camera?

Fenrick scrubbed a hand over his face in frustration.

"We need to ask the shifter," Fenrick said through gritted teeth.

"Where is he?" I asked the group.

The guy in the middle pointed to a cell a couple down from Karma. The man was lying on the cot in what looked like sleep.

"Was he checked by a healer?" Aurelia frowned.

"No, he's been like that since we found him. I think he was drugged," the warlock said.

"Someone get a damn healer!" I barked.

Fenrick waved me off. "No need. I am a decent healer by Fae standards."

"I'm not exactly happy with Fae standards at the moment."

"Watch it," Aurelia said. "He's on our side."

"Plus, your mate is Fae." Fenrick held his hands over the man's body, and they glowed green with healing magic.

The man moaned and blinked his eyes open.

"Where am I?" he mumbled. "This doesn't look like the human jail."

"That was no human jail," the warlock said.

Did he really think it was a supernatural jail? But we just didn't have those, for the most part.

"What's your name?" I asked the shifter.

His eyes locked on mine for only a second before he averted his gaze.

"Taryn, my king," he said with his head bowed low.

"So you do know who I am then?" I asked, raising a brow.

"Yes, I am very old even though I don't look it. I knew your father before his passing all those years ago," he said sadly.

"We will get back to that in a minute." I glanced at Aurelia as her shoulders stiffened with his words.

"What is it you wish to know?" Taryn asked.

"How does someone as old as you get caught on camera shifting and attacking people?" There had to be a good explanation. I didn't want this man dead, especially after the way we retrieved him.

"I don't know. There was something strange about the whole incident." He shook his head.

"What do you mean, strange?" Aurelia stepped closer to the bars.

I pulled her back gently even though she scowled at me. Just because I didn't want him dead didn't mean I trusted him close to my mate.

"I mean that I was just walking by the shop and there was a strange scent in the air. It was almost a chemical aroma. I became irrationally angry then shifted." He scooted forward on the small cot.

"A chemical smell? That sounds more like the humans than the Fae," I rubbed a hand across my chin.

"But why would the humans expose us? They don't want mass hysteria." Aurelia leaned forward again.

She shuffled her feet and chewed her lip in thought.

"What do the Fae have to do with any of this?" Taryn asked with a growl.

He sniffed the air and cocked his head to the side as he stared between Fenrick and Aurelia.

"That is my mate and her guardian. They will be respected!" I barked at the man.

His glare turned to curiosity then he averted his eyes.

Good. I needed more information from him and if he thought they were wicked Fae, then he wouldn't be as helpful as he was currently being.

"The Fae want to enslave us all now." I leaned my back against the wall and brought Aurelia with me into the circle of my arms again.

"It wasn't bad enough that they exiled us, but now they want to enslave us too?" Taryn scoffed.

"Apparently not. And this has their dirty dealings all over it." I stared the shifter down. "How did you get on their list?"

"Even after he was disgraced and executed, I was a supporter of your father. I was loud and attempted to rise up against our oppressors. They have long memories, it seems." He stood abruptly.

I tensed along with Fenrick, who took a step to block Aurelia from the shifter's view. Once a protector, always a protector.

"He wasn't dead," Aurelia's whisper was choked on a sob.

Taryn's gaze snapped to hers. There was anger in his eyes. The scent of his fury filled the space and I nearly choked on the sour stench.

"You dare lie? I watched his execution with my own eyes." He took a threatening step forward, vibrating with rage.

"Watch your tone with the princess, mutt. I saw him alive and well and stuck in a cage next to hers." Fenrick stomped to the bars.

This conversation was devolving fast. We'd gotten almost everything we needed from the shifter, but something wasn't adding up.

"Easy, Fenrick. He can't get to my mate, nor would he. Would you, Taryn?" I raised a brow.

"No, my king. I just don't believe it," he whispered.

"Whoever they killed was not the king. I made friends with Nickolas in that cell." Aurelia turned and buried her face in my chest as tears filled her eyes.

"This isn't the point." I rubbed Aurelia's back in soothing circles. "What happened at the jail? You were unconscious until Fenrick healed you."

"I was still shifting uncontrollably until they knocked me out with a needle. Then I woke up here." He glanced around the holding area.

"What the fuck did the humans come up with that could make a shifter go crazy like that, and why? Did the Fae have something to do with how that was made?" I asked no one in particular.

"I think we are getting ahead of ourselves here, and I don't want to discuss plans in front of the other prisoners." Aurelia eyed Karma warily.

"Agreed." Fenrick nodded, still glaring at Taryn. "We should head back to the office and devise a plan. We can't really do anything about this mystery right now."

I nudged Aurelia, and she turned to leave without a backward glance at either prisoner.

She was getting the royal act down pretty quickly for someone who never had anything. I grinned. She would be my queen one day. I was glad she would live up to the title in every way.

When we got into the elevator, I reached to push the button for the top when she grabbed my arm.

"Can we check on Freya first?" she asked with tears pooling in her eyes.

I could deny my mate nothing. What happened to the ruthless leader of the Syndicate? I used to be cold and unfeeling. This woman was going to be the death of that image.

I nodded my head and pushed the button for the infirmary instead.

Aurelia raced out of the elevator as soon as the doors opened, and I followed behind her to the room in which we'd left Freya. Fiona sat on the small cot with her head in her hands, silently sobbing.

"No," Aurelia gasped. "Please no."

"What?" I asked, searching the room for the sprite.

Where was she? She had to be there. Where was Magna?

"What's going on?" I croaked. "Where is Freya?"

Fiona sniffled and turned her watery gaze on me. Her eyes

were red-rimmed from crying and I swore to the gods if this was one of their pranks, I would strangle them myself.

"She was injured too badly. Nothing that Magna did helped," Fiona sobbed.

I was shaking my head, denying the truth before the words were even fully out of her mouth. "No."

Magna walked into the doorway and stopped, her expression grave. "It wasn't that. They tainted her blood with something that would not allow her to heal. They experimented on her."

"They did what?" Aurelia gasped.

She sat like a stone on the bed next to Fiona, who was still quietly sobbing.

"It's like the shifter, but different?" I ran a hand down my face.

"It would seem so," Magna said softly.

What the fuck was the Council doing? Why were they experimenting on their own damn people? They were fucking monsters.

"I don't care how long it takes, or what I have to do, I will see the Council fall," I vowed.

Aurelia stared at me sadly, probably already knowing who would make them all pay. This had all been firmly on her shoulders and I had a feeling it was only the beginning of her trials.

"I'll kill him for this," she whispered.

"I would rather you not have blood on your hands." I pulled her into my arms.

"Too late. My soul is already stained with the blood of my enemies and my friends. I will end them all for this and for Nickolas." A single tear traced down her cheek before she swiped at it angrily.

"Let's go get this damn book so we can end this once and for all." I pulled her from the room.

We didn't need to be in there anymore. The scent of death permeated the air and made my oversensitive nose twitch.

"Fenrick!" Aurelia called to the guard. "Find my father. We are going to need his help if there are any problems."

Fenrick nodded and pushed the button to the elevator. I wrapped my arms around Aurelia and brushed a kiss across her forehead.

"Everything is moving so fast, but it feels like I'm standing still." She laid her head on my chest.

Magna walked out of the room, leaving Fiona to her grief.

"You found your memories, Princess?" she asked.

"I did, and I understand so much more now." Aurelia nodded.

"Just by touch alone you can grant access to Faery," Magna said with a watery smile.

"What do you mean?" Aurelia asked. "I can't sift."

"You don't need to be able to sift. Just touch me and I will be able to sift to Faery independent of you. I have seen it." Magna smiled.

"So, I can take Grey?" she asked hopefully.

"Yes." Magna patted her on the arm.

"This changes everything." I squeezed Aurelia tighter.

The elevator dinged and the doors opened. Fenrick and the shadow king stood inside. We rushed through the doors with Magna on our heels.

"We need to go to the parking garage. We can't sift inside the wards." I hit the down button. We were going to Faery for the first time in centuries. I know I shouldn't smile so soon after my dear friend's death, but the thought of going home even for a short time made me happy.

Turning to the woman responsible for it all, I crashed my lips to hers in a bruising kiss. She made this possible.

"Grey, my father," she whispered against my lips when I wouldn't let her go.

"I was just thanking my mate for being the best thing that ever happened to the realms." I grinned.

"You're crazy." She pulled away from me, and I let her go reluctantly.

The elevator doors opened, and we stepped out into the empty garage.

We didn't quite know what we were facing or what would happen when we got there, but we were going home, and I would have faced the doors of death to get that chance again.

CHAPTER 25
Aurelia

I crouched behind a bush and stared at the castle. The trees were waving urgently. It wasn't as weird now that I knew about them doing the same when I was a child.

My father crouched next to me, glaring at the men patrolling the building. "What are the Council's soldiers doing guarding my castle?"

"I don't know, but we need to get out of here," I said just as softly. "The trees are trying to warn us away."

Grey gazed up at the trees with a frown, and we backed away from the tree line.

The Council was clearly moving to take over anyone that opposed them, and my father's kingdom was firmly in the opposition.

"What happened to my soldiers?" he asked as we moved swiftly through the trees.

Fenrick paused and shook his head. "I'm guessing that any who didn't swear allegiance to the Council were either killed or sent to the dungeons."

"That will make things exceedingly more difficult in the battle ahead." I chewed my lip nervously.

Grey squeezed my hand, and I peered up at him. Even with the grim news of our lack of army, there was a light in his eyes I hadn't seen before.

He was happy to be back in his home, even if the state of it was terrible and oppressive.

"We'll fix it," Grey murmured. "Let's just get the book first."

"It's close to the portal," I said.

I was so glad I remembered where I stashed it now but when we sifted, we missed the mark by a mile. Father said it was by design, in case any Council soldiers were near it.

The trees swayed the opposite direction of the portal and I cringed. They wanted us to run the other way, but we needed the book.

"I think they're at the portal." I scanned the trees. "They are frantic that we get out of here."

"We'll have to fight then, daughter. There is no other way but retrieving the book," my father mumbled.

"I know, I just like having the early warning system, so we're all on alert." I stepped on a twig, and a loud snap filled the air.

I cringed. That was not what I wanted to do.

Way to go, Aurelia. You could have just alerted the whole forest to your presence.

Fenrick turned sharply and stared at me. It wasn't like me as a child when I moved so silently between the trees.

I asked the trees to remove the sticks from our path and they silently agreed. Placing a palm on the trunk of the nearest tree, I poured a little magic into it as a thank you.

They listened to me. But not because I demanded things, because I asked them nicely and then thanked them when they agreed.

The tree pulsed with fear, and I attempted to reassure it. It was afraid for me. They all seemed to be, as the branches reached for me, urging me the other direction.

"They're scared," I whispered. "They are saying there are a lot of bad men in that direction."

Grey cocked a brow. "How many?"

"They have no concept of numbers, just many. They feel angry and violent." I shook my head and continued on quietly.

"Over this hill," Fenrick whispered, pointing at the small hill in front of us. "The portal is on the other side."

"We need to keep low. Being on higher ground is where you want to be in battle, but it can also put a target on your back." Father squared his shoulders, only succeeding in making him bigger not smaller.

As we came to the crest of the hill, a clearing was visible in front of us. The Council guards filled the space.

"What are they doing?" I asked. They were waiting for something as they stared at the portal in perfect formation.

"They are preparing for war." Grey said and clenched his fist around the hilt of the sword in his sheath.

I hadn't even known he could use a sword. I'd thought he just shifted and killed that way. I didn't dare admit how sexy it made him look in battle armor.

I needed to get my head out of the gutter and back into the task at hand.

"What are we going to do?" I pointed to the tree that once had the hollow close to the portal. "It's in that tree."

"In the tree?" Fenrick frowned. "Is that how you always hid from me?"

"So not the time, Fenrick." I grinned.

"I never could figure it out," he mumbled to himself.

I held in my giggle but just barely. I squeaked as the ground rumbled beneath me and a root shot from the earth and wrapped itself around my waist firmly.

"What the fuck?" I whispered, but I felt no malice or ill intent from the roots.

Grey had his sword out and was about to start hacking at it when a hole opened up in the ground. My stomach jolted and as I fell, a scream tore from my lips.

Fuck, that was damn subtle.

The tree root caught me halfway down and another hole opened in front of me. What the hell was going on? Were the trees helping me sneak past the army at the portal?

Calling on my magic, it crackled along my palm, lighting the dark tunnel before me. This was insane but I reached out to the root with my free hand and sent my thanks.

I traveled down the tunnel quietly behind a root that reached out, beckoning me forward.

I stumbled on a pebble in the hard-packed dirt. A root sprung from the wall next to me and wrapped around my arm, balancing me.

Weird, but very cool.

The clang of metal reached my ears from somewhere above my head, and a mournful howl broke through the din of battle.

What the fuck was going on? Were Grey and my father okay? Were they fighting for their lives?

Panic seized me as I picked up my pace. The tree root beckoned me more frantically. I ran as fast as my feet would take me, begging the trees to help them in any way they could, but unsure if they could hear me.

I had to believe I didn't put them all in danger with my scream of terror. I had to focus on the task at hand and pray to any gods that were listening that they would make it out alive.

The root led me down a second tunnel and silence filled the space.

Were they still fighting up there, or did they flee?

I hoped beyond hope that they had fled the giant army that had been waiting at the portal in battle formation.

I needed them all to get out of this alive. I'd lost too much already.

At the end of the tunnel there was only a root and hard-packed earth. The root wrapped around me tightly again and it lifted me in the air, the earth opening up into the hollow of the giant oak.

It was smaller than I remembered, but the bushes still covered the entrance, keeping it hidden. I peeked out of the bush and Ronaldo stood in front of the large army. Four people were on their knees in front of him.

He grinned down at them with a maliciousness only he could express. Grey struggled with the bonds, his eyes scanning the forest and his head held high.

"You will never find her!" he yelled, but a tear streaked his cheek.

Did he think I was dead? Is that why he told Ronaldo he would never find me?

I sat back on my heels and glanced between the others. My father's expression was thunderous, but he took had his chin up.

"The new realm order has already begun," Ronaldo said smugly. "And you four will be the first of the slaves."

"No," I whispered so quietly no one would hear over the shouts of victory by the soldiers of the army as they clamped magic cuffs on my friends and family.

A root nudged me from behind and I turned. An old, gold book sat in a bush of burnt orange leaves. It was the book I had been looking for, but now that everyone was captured did it really matter?

I couldn't sift and my only transport was a portal currently blocked by the enemy army.

I grabbed the book and it buzzed with recognition.

This was most definitely the right book. I turned back to the army, wanting desperately to be with Grey and the others, but I was our only chance of survival now.

I eyed the root and nodded back to the way we came. I had to get out of here and that was the only way.

I would get my friends and family back and end the elder Council even if I had to die in the process.

"Can you take me to the dungeons without being seen?" I whispered to the root.

An idea was forming. If I was going to defeat an army, I needed to free an army of my own.

I would be the princess I was born to be. I would be their queen and lead them ito victory.

I just needed to rescue them from my father's dungeon first.

∽

The final book in the Wicked Fae trilogy is coming soon!
Pre-order: https://books2read.com/chosenfae

Printed in Great Britain
by Amazon